Intro

Though all the characters in Hope Remains are fictional, the story is built around an actual event which happened in the Dutch Fork area of South Carolina in the mid eighteenth century.

The story has a form of time travel which involves sending pulses of light as Morse code messages back in time through a black hole. Humans don't travel, but light does, affecting the present day. The details of the development of the time machine were covered in Beyond Time, the first book in the series.

Hope Remains stands alone and can be fully understood without <u>Beyond Time</u>. However, if you want the back story and the development of characters such as Peter, Alfred, Jimmy and Stephen, <u>Beyond Time</u> will fill in the details for you.

What you're about to experience is a weaving together of two separate but related stories which are set in motion by the discovery of two undelivered letters by kids playing in a run-down cabin in the woods.

I hope you enjoy the story and can relate to the journeys of the characters involved.

Rob Buck

ONE

Irmo, South Carolina

Bubba's stringy hair swung down over his eyes as it had done dozens of times that day. As he looped his greasy locks around his ears, he walked casually across Highway 6, a two-lane rural highway, toward the parked mail truck.

The carrier had stopped at the Corner Pantry at exactly 10:30 for a cup of coffee and one of their famous sausage biscuits, just as MB had said he would.

Bubba's job was to make sure two letters sent by Jacob Younginer were not delivered. He wasn't exactly sure why, but that was what he was going to do.

Looking inside the building, he saw the lanky mailman, pondering whether to use French Vanilla or straight half-and-half in his coffee.

Keeping his head low as MB had instructed, Bubba peeked inside the mail truck and spotted groups of letters neatly stacked.

"One of Jacob's letters is being delivered to Selwood and the other to Weed Drive," MB had said. "Grab them and destroy them."

Bubba wasn't sure who MB really was. They originally met at the *Dam Bar and Grill* on the other side of Lake Murray from his house. MB had offered to keep him supplied with beer if he'd run some errands. MB was obsessed with this Jacob fellow.

Bubba knelt beside the truck, partially hidden from view by a white sedan. He leaned through the opening in the driver's side of the mail truck and began thumbing through the stacks of letters sorted by street. He found the Weed Drive stack. Sweat dropped from his brow as he shuffled through the stack of letters.

Inside the Pantry, the owner of the white sedan was collecting her change as the mailman stepped up to pay.

Bubba saw the Pantry door open and a teenage girl chewing gum and talking on her cell phone headed his way. Bubba had to act quickly. He tossed the letters from Weed Drive he'd already examined back in the stack and kept five or six he hadn't looked at yet. He could only hope the letter to Sarah Jenkins was among them. Then he spotted the word 'Selwood' on a letter at the top of another bundle of letters in the mail tray. It was from Jacob Younginer.

By then the girl ended her call and emerged between the vehicles, Bubba grabbed the Selwood letter, added it to the others and rolled his grossly fat body out of the opening of the mail truck and crawled to the rear of the two vehicles to avoid being seen.

"Excuse you!" the girl yelled at him.

Bubba struggled to his knees and then to his feet as the mailman exited the Pantry.

"What were you doing to my car?" the girl yelled, as Bubba started running across the parking lot toward Highway 6.

Bubba rumbled across the road and into the woods on the other side, ignoring the car that slammed on its brakes to avoid hitting him.

Bubba labored to reach the old two-room shack in the woods. He squeezed through the door and collapsed in a mound of greasy blubber and stench. As he panted, sweat poured down his forehead and dripped onto the musty wooden floor planks.

After catching his breath, he flipped through the letters. The first few were bills.

"Bingo!" Bubba wiped the sweat off his face with his forearm and held up the letter. "Sorry Sarah Jenkins, whoever you are, you won't be getting this letter from Mr. Jacob Younginer!"

He struggled to his feet and called MB.

"I don't care what you do with them as long as you destroy them!" MB said after Bubba informed him. "I already know what they say."

Bubba, almost asked him why, but remembered MB's burst of anger the last time he asked a question. He'd gone into a cussing rant, letting Bubba know that it was none of his blanking business.

Bubba stuffed the letters between some slats in the floor. He thought he might want to come back and read them one day.

Almost Three Years Later

"Come on Cassie," urged Daniel, "We're getting close."

"I'm hurrying." Cassie shouted back to her older brother. "Where is this place? Shouldn't we have gotten to it by now?"

"It's right up the hill and to the right."

After a few more moments of fighting through the thick brush, Daniel cried, "Here it is!"

The 14- and 10-year-old siblings came into view of an old shack, barely visible, in the depths of the woods behind their house.

"This place looks creepy," said Cassie, a petite, beautiful girl. She stopped in dead stride, her deep, blue eyes staring tentatively at the old two-room building, which was in desperate need of repair.

Daniel, a solidly built boy on the verge of manhood, stepped over a fallen tree and held back a handful of overgrown vine tendrils for his sister to pass through. He watched her stare timidly at the old shack that stood before them.

"I knew you'd be too chicken to follow through with it," Daniel chided. "Come on, there could be some really cool stuff in there," he persuaded, as he walked slowly to the door of the cabin.

"How did you find this place, Danny? You can barely see it through all these vines," Cassie asked, ignoring his jibe.

Cassie had a love, hate relationship with her brown curly headed brother. She couldn't help but marvel at his care free, adventurous spirit, but ever since their dad left the year before, Danny had relentlessly picked on her. It hurt her all the more because of how much she admired him.

"Buster followed me the other day when I cut through the woods to the Pantry," Danny answered. "He ran off the path toward this area chasing a squirrel. Then I noticed that side wall through the bushes."

"It looks like no one cares about this place at all. It's a wreck." Cassie remarked as she turned her head to ease through the space between the vines, trying carefully to avoid the small thorns.

Once Cassie was clear, Daniel let go of the vines and moved past her, approaching the two-step front porch of the abandoned shack. He eased one foot onto the first step, which looked weathered, but felt solid. The second step creaked loud enough to stir some birds, but held firm.

Daniel slid across the porch avoiding a section with two rotten planks.

"Let's go, Cassie," Daniel called back to his sister as he reached for the dingy brass door knob. It was chipped and dented, but he easily turned it.

Cassie hesitantly joined her brother as he pushed the door open and stepped in.

"Wow!" Daniel yelled, as he surveyed his surroundings.

"What is it?" Cassie asked overcoming her fears and sliding through the door.

The walls were made of plain plank boards and the inside was scattered with debris. Several windows were broken and in the back room a small tree branch protruded over the floor.

"What do you mean "Wow?" What's so great about a bunch of old newspapers, letters, and cans?"

Cassie looked over at Daniel and immediately got her answer. In the corner, behind the door, were dozens of old bottles, including an old Pepsi bottle with the rare white oval label.

"Now I see. I know where those bottles are going to end up."

"You're right." Daniel responded, as he began to examine his find. "They'll be a great addition to my bottle collection. Look at this one!" Daniel held up a dark blue bottle shaped like a tear drop with a base and cork stuffed in the top.

"Must have been a pill bottle," observed Cassie. "Hey, check out the dates on these newspapers. Some are almost twenty years old. Here's one from the month and year mom and dad got married."

"How do you know that?"

"Mom, told me the other day," Cassie replied. "She was sad about not making it to their 20th anniversary."

"I hope they get a divorce," Daniel said.

"How can you say that, Danny?" Cassie said, raising her voice.

"Look at this newspaper," Daniel responded, ignoring Cassie's emotional outburst. "This one's from two days ago!"

"Oh no! Do you think someone actually lives here?" Cassie asked.

"Could be, or maybe they're trespassing," Danny chuckled.

"Like us," Cassie realized. "I'm scared Danny. Please, let's go."

"We will soon," Daniel responded, already examining the next bottle.

Before long Cassie's fears eased and the siblings were lost in the junk of the old cabin. In the back room, they discovered many old Time and Life magazines, which they brought back into the front room.

Glancing up from flipping through a magazine, Cassie was mesmerized by a cluster of dust dancing slowly though a sun beam toward the floor. The particles disappeared between the floor planks, and she caught a glance of something white.

She crawled over on her knees and peered between the slats, trying to make out what it was.

"What are you doing, Cassie?" Daniel laid down an old newspaper and walked over to observe.

"There are some papers or something under the floor here, but I can't tell what they are." Cassie backed away for Daniel to see.

"I can't tell either," said Daniel.

Daniel stood up and looked around the room. He spotted a broken shovel near the back door and grabbed it. He then proceeded to pry the floor planks apart widening the gap and breaking off some of the rotted wood, but the opening wasn't wide enough for him to reach the treasure.

"Cassie, come see if you can reach one of them. I bet your arm is thin enough."

"No way," Cassie answered vehemently. "There could be spiders and rats down there!"

"Spiders and rats?"

Instead of combating her fears with logic, Daniel, stood up and took his frustration out on the next floor plank. He smashed it hard with the heel of his shoe. The plank snapped in two and fell to the dirt below the floor.

"If you aren't going to help, then you're not going to be able to see what's here!" Daniel snapped irritably. He stuck his arm in the exposed floor space and grabbed the papers.

"These are letters!" Daniel exclaimed with excitement. "And they've never even been opened."

"Let me see!" Cassie insisted as she approached her brother.

"No way; these are mine. You should've helped me."

"But I saw them first!"

Ignoring his sister's plea, Daniel examined his prize. He liked the racing stamps on the letters and noticed they were postmarked almost three years ago. He grabbed the top one and sat down, securing the others safe from Cassie's reach under his leg, below where his winter jeans had been cut off for the summer.

It was addressed to Sarah Jenkins 13 Weed Drive, Irmo, SC, 29063. It was from Jacob Younginer at 518 Ashley River Court in Charleston, SC 29812.

"I wonder why it was never opened?" he mumbled, ripping open the letter and starting to read it. He was too curious to care that Cassie had slipped beside him, her shoulder length blond hair now slightly ruffling in the gentle air flow of a broken window.

"Should we be reading this?" Cassie asked.

Ignoring her question, Daniel began to read out loud:

My Dear Sarah,

Words cannot express how sorry I am to have caused you such pain. You offered me your battered heart and gave me everything you had. Like a fool, I didn't realize how much

Suddenly Daniel stopped.

"What was that?" Cassie asked, fear gripping her as she reached for Daniel's arm.

Right outside the cabin was the unmistakable crunch of leaves followed by the sound of footsteps.

"Who's in there?" bellowed a male voice from the porch.

TWO

Cassie screamed and stood up, staring at the doorway.

"Come on!" Daniel yelled, pulling her arm in the direction of the back room.

They stumbled across bottles, cans and newspapers and exited the front room just as Bubba's rotund body busted through the front door.

"Hey, what are you kids doing in here?" Bubba yelled, as he spotted them. He tripped over what was left of an old chair and almost fell.

Righting himself, he stumbled into the back room in time to catch a glimpse of Daniel jumping out of the window he'd just helped his sister out of.

Bubba's eyes followed them through the broken windows as he made his way back to the front room. Then he froze as he noticed the broken floor planks. He staggered through the clutter and peered into the hole. They were gone; those letters MB had him steal a few years ago. He'd almost forgotten about them.

Fear gripped him as he thought back to his last encounter with MB. It was several weeks ago, when MB pulled up in front of his mom's place late one evening. He was dropping off some beer money.

As he took the envelope from him, Bubba couldn't help noticing a gun beside MB on the front seat and a very frightened lady sitting next to him. As MB held the gun so that Bubba could see it, he told him he was moving to Charleston. He told Bubba to let him know of anything suspicious. Bubba wasn't sure what he was to be suspicious about, but he knew MB was serious.

Bubba felt threatened and wished he'd never gotten mixed up with MB and his crazy obsessions, even if it did yield a steady flow of petty cash.

The image of the woman and her desperate look haunted him. He didn't want to think of what MB would do to him if those letters he was supposed to have destroyed ever surfaced.

Bubba busted through the front door, rumbled down the steps and into the woods after the kids. He had to get those letters back.

Daniel and Cassie didn't stop running until they crossed the bridge at the back of their property.

"Do you think we lost him?" Cassie asked as Daniel sat down on the bridge and dangled his feet over the small creek below.

"That guy's so fat I'm sure he gave up the chase before the first bridge," Daniel said, pulling out the letter to Sarah Jenkins and beginning to read where he left off.

Her curiosity about the letter overshadowing her fear of the man chasing them, Cassie sat down beside her brother on the bridge. "Could you read it out loud Danny?"

"Yeah I guess so. Let's see... *Like a fool, I...*"

"Can you start it over, please?"

"Okay," Daniel agreed reluctantly.

'My Dear Sarah,

Words cannot express how sorry I am to have caused you such pain. You offered me your battered heart and gave me everything you had. Like a fool, I didn't realize how much you mean to me until too late. I was selfish. Once again, I was thinking only of me.

It's been three days since you left here in tears and they've been the longest days of my life. I guess sometimes, you really don't realize what you have until you lose it. I was scared. After so many years of being a bachelor, I was afraid of commitment. Cindy means nothing to me.

After only a few days without you, I've realized how much I am desperately in love with you. If you'll have me back, I'd like to be with you the rest of my life. But I know I've broken your heart.

If you can forgive me, please write me back, or call me.

If I don't hear from you, I completely understand. You said you never wanted to see me again and that may still be how you feel. I will honor your decision

.

With all my love,

Jacob

In the signature line after his name was Jacob's address and phone number.

"So, this guy tried to make up with his girlfriend years ago," Danny, observed. "I bet he ended up with the Cindy girl."

"You don't know that, Danny!" Cassie replied, trying to hide her emotions.

Looking over at Cassie, Daniel noticed she was wiping a tear from her eye.

"Oh good grief, Cassie, don't be such a sissy."

"I don't care what you think! He's sharing his heart with her, it's so sweet. We should take this letter to Sarah. It says she lives on Weed, the next street over. Maybe we can save their relationship."

"If he hasn't heard back from her by now, I'm sure he's given up." Daniel snorted.

"I bet he still loves her and she needs to know it!" Cassie erupted.

"I think it's a waste of time," Daniel replied. "I'm trashing this one and looking at the others!"

"Let's at least take the letter to the post office," Cassie pleaded as she stood up from her seat on the bridge and looked down at Daniel. "They are supposed to make sure every letter gets delivered."

Daniel ignored his sister and started opening the next letter.

Seeing her opportunity, Cassie snatched the letters from Daniel and took off across the yard toward their house, screaming loudly, "Mom!"

Daniel grabbed at the letters as Cassie fled, but was only able to hang onto the one he had started opening. He considered running after his sister, but given the fuss she was making, he was content to sit down and examine his remaining prize.

The letter, with no street number, was addressed to Dr. William Shuler, Selwood, Irmo SC, 29063. The return address was the same as the letter to Sarah: Jacob Younginer, 518 Ashley River Court, Charleston, SC 29812.

"Wow," Daniel said to himself, as he finished opening the letter. "I bet it was mailed the same day."

Unfolding the letter, he began to read:

Dr. Shuler,

You don't know me, but I believe I have information which may be of interest to you. In looking through family documents in the attic of my deceased grandfather's home I found the enclosed map. It points to a spot in the Broad River floodplain on Hope Creek which flows into the main river.

The map itself seemed to be of no consequence and I set it aside as I continued to pour through the papers I found locked in an old chest. However, I then came across the attached letter dated June 17th, 1940. It is from one of my grandfather's brothers, a man named Luke Younginer. I can't tell who the letter was addressed to.

I can only hope my grandfather wasn't involved and was only the keeper of family documents. It seems from the tone of the letter that at least my Great Uncle Luke was up to no good.

Since Hope was capitalized in the attached document, I wondered if Hope might be a name. So, I did some research. My research led to a reference book at the Lake Murray Welcome Center, near the dam. In the book named, <u>The Legends of Dutch Fork</u>, I found an article about the Hope Creek Mystery. The article is about the discovery of 50 to 60 graves in the river bed in 1919. All of these graves have stones marked with the same year, 1749. Almost all of them had the first name and the letter H. On some of the markers, however, the name 'Hope' can clearly be recognized. The article gave a general description of the grave markers. The map I found in that chest describes the exact spot.

To this day it is a mystery as to why all those people died the same year, but what I've found seems to point to some sort of massacre. I hope, I'm wrong Dr. Shuler.

If you follow the map, you might find the gravestones. They will most likely be covered by the river sediment so you may have to dig a bit. Perhaps what I've uncovered here will help bring light to this long-time mystery.

Because of personal issues in my life right now, I lack the emotional energy to do more research or to even turn these documents over to the police. I have told no one else about these discoveries.

According to local records, your mother's maiden name was Hope. In fact, she was the last person in our area with that last name. It is for this reason I pass this information to you. Do with it as you please.

Sincerely,

Jacob Younginer

Daniel folded the letter and studied the map. He recognized street names from his school bus route, but the map itself confused him.

He slowly unfolded the brittle, yellowed letter that was also attached and began to read:

June 17th, 1940

Keep the map hidden. It marks the beginning of the crusade to wipe out the invaders. Continue what was begun and wipe them out until no Hope remains.

Luke

Puzzled, but intrigued, Daniel carefully re-folded the weathered letter and slid it and the other two documents back into the envelope. In deep thought, he slid the envelope into his pocket and headed toward his house.

Just across the creek and to the left of the bridge, Bubba stood in the shadows of dusk and watched Daniel walk up the narrow path to his house.

Downtown Columbia, South Carolina

Hank Eagan pulled into the garage of his patio home next to the park. The weekend was fast approaching, but it offered little relief from the loneliness he felt. At least he could look forward to some of his favorite Thursday night TV shows

He closed the garage door and entered the kitchen. The monotonous drone of the humming appliances was like an audible expression of his life. Like every other day the countertops were spotless, the floors were swept clean, and there was no clutter.

For the first few months after leaving his family, he felt relaxed. He could handle the stress of being a computer programming supervisor much better than he could handle being a husband and a father.

But as the months rolled by, the peace he first felt from the quiet of an empty, ordered house had turned into pure loneliness. As he sat watching Wheel of Fortune, he wondered if the coming weekend would yield anything different than mindlessly roaming through bars and restaurants.

It had been almost a year since he left. He tried to see his kids when he could, but seeing them just depressed him more. His visits reminded him of a life that could have been.

He opened the refrigerator and took out some pizza. He sprinkled on loads of parmesan cheese and placed a few slices in the microwave.

He stood there staring at the time rolling backwards on the digital display.

His thoughts turned to his wife, Tammy. They used to have so much in common. They had been a champion husband and wife pool team, often blowing out the competition in tournaments. If they weren't playing pool they were enjoying parties with their friends and having a blast. Their relationship was marked by laughter.

Then there were the kids. Daniel was born first, and then Cassie. He loved them, but he knew his actions didn't show it. With his job taking fifty-five plus hours a week and all the other duties of running a home, he hadn't really made time for them.

When he realized how much his absence was hurting them, especially Daniel, he tried to focus on them more. Cassie was open to this change and they had some great times together: walking in the woods, going to movies, and reading. But for Daniel the damage was already done. He would not even look Hank in the eyes and barely spoke to him. Daniel and his dad were constantly at odds and once almost exchanged punches. At another time, Hank squeezed Daniel's arm so hard it left a mark for over a week.

Now, every time Hank tried to reach out to Daniel and make amends, his attempts were rejected. Hank didn't know how to handle this and grew angrier at each incident. Their relationship had reached toxic levels.

The microwave beeped. Hank poured a beer and took the slices of pizza outside on the porch. It was a fantastic view. He could see the buildings of downtown Columbia against the darkening blue sky. Once providing hours of relaxation, the steady roaring of the park's two-story-high waterfall provided little relief now.

He was beginning to realize that no matter where he was, what he was doing, or who he was with, nothing changed the loneliness he felt inside.

As he munched on the pepperoni pizza and drank his beer, his thoughts drifted back to Tammy. In some ways, he was happy she'd become so serious about religion. He'd noticed a huge change in her, especially when it came to her bouts of depression. But it all seemed out of balance. He felt left out.

Hank popped the last of the pizza into his mouth and finished the rest of his beer as he got up to get more of both. He adjusted his belt out a notch as he walked back to the kitchen and thought that he needed to start jogging again soon.

Back on the porch, he remembered the day when he packed his things to leave. Cassie was clinging to her stuffed kitty and wailing uncontrollably. Daniel retreated angrily to his room. Tammy gently pulled Cassie to her side, trying to hold and comfort her.

By now the last of the sun fell behind the buildings. A gray dusk settled and seemed to mirror Hank's mood. He lit a cigarette. He puffed hard and slowly exhaled, taking in the cloud canopy that engulfed him.

He heard his cell phone ring and tapped his blue-tooth to answer it without checking who it was.

"Hello," he said.

"Hank," Tammy's voice sounded on the other end, "we've got an issue here."

"What's wrong this time?"

"The kids have found some letters in the woods and we need your help."

"Letters, what do you mean?"

"They found some unopened letters in an old shack in the back of the woods and Cassie really wants to deliver one of them. It's addressed to a house nearby, but I don't want her roaming around alone."

"Why is that our business?" Hank snapped impatiently.

"It's our business because our daughter wants to deliver it. I have to go in early to work tomorrow so I can't take her."

"Tomorrow! What's the urgency?"

"Here," Tammy said, handing the phone to Cassie. "Talk to your father."

"Daddy?" Cassie began. "Can you please take me? The letter is a proposal that was never delivered."

"Cassie, can't it wait until I see you next. I have to work tomorrow, you know."

"I know, Daddy. Never mind."

Cassie handed the phone back to her mom, looking down. She was used to being disappointed. Like everything else she'd been hit with lately, she tried to allow the hurt to bounce off her heart and not land.

"Okay, thanks again for being there for us, Hank," Tammy said tersely as she took the phone from Cassie. "I was trying to give you a chance to be there for one of your kids."

"Good grief, Tammy. Why are you making such a big deal over a letter?" Hank asked, raising his voice. But Tammy had already hung up.

Hank returned to his beer, pizza and TV. Before long, guilt overshadowed him and he called back and agreed to pick Cassie up the next morning at 7:30.

"Be sure she's ready then," he urged. "I don't want to be late for work."

"Of course you don't," Tammy said.

She paused, but then said, "Thank you."

THREE

Irmo, South Carolina

"Cassie, you really shouldn't have opened this letter." Hank said as they pulled out of their driveway the next morning.

"I know, Daddy," Cassie agreed, fighting the temptation to point out that it was Daniel who opened it.

"Are these all the letters?" Hank asked.

"No, Danny has another one," Cassie said as they turned onto Weed Drive. "We had an argument and I snatched these away from him, but he held onto one. I saw that it was from Jacob Younginer, but I didn't see who it was written to."

"Well that's interesting," said Hank. "We'll need to get that one too."

"Daddy, what if Sarah's not home?" Cassie asked as she started to look at the numbers written on the mailboxes.

"Then I guess we can just put it in her mailbox. What was that house number again?"

"Thirteen," Cassie answered without looking at the envelope.

"This is it," Hank said as he slowed down and turned into a gravel driveway at the edge of an open field.

The brick house was small and painted white, emphasizing the rusted wagon wheel leaning against it. The roof was green with matching shutters.

Though Hank had lived one street over his whole married life, he never really noticed the house. If he'd learned anything over his months alone, he realized how much life he'd rushed past. Hurrying had only gained him a broken marriage, an angry son, and a whole lot of heartache. He was trying to slow down and be present in the moment. He wished he'd determined to do this years before.

"You ready Daddy?"

"Yea," Hank answered, aroused from his day dream. They got out of the car and walked across the gravel driveway to a stone walk way leading to the front door.

When they got there, Hank rang the doorbell. After a long moment, the door cracked open as far as the inside restraining chain would allow.

"May I help you?" asked an elderly lady.

"Yes," Hank replied. "We're looking for Sarah Jenkins."

"What has that woman done? Someone else was looking for her a while back. She hasn't lived here for months."

"She hasn't done anything as far as I know," Hank answered. "We have a letter for her."

"And it's almost three years old," Cassie piped in.

"Sweetie, I'm sure the lady doesn't care about that," Hank said.

"I wish I could help you," the lady said as she unchained the door and stepped outside. "She rented the house before me, but that's all I know about her. Well, that and she must have had a ton of cats; still finding fur balls."

"Okay, thanks ma'am," Hank turned to leave. "We'll take it to the post office so they can forward it to her."

"Hold on a minute," the lady said. "I just remembered there was a friend of hers who came by to pick up her mail soon after she moved out. He left his card and told me to call him if more came. Let me see if I can find it. Just a minute."

The lady returned with a business card and handed it to Hank. "His name is Dr. Anderson," she said, "Said he's a professor at the University of South Carolina. Maybe he can help you find her."

Hank thanked the lady and headed to the car with Cassie.

"This is getting very complicated, Cassie. I'm going to take this letter, along with the bills, to the post office and be done with it. Tell Daniel I'll need the one he has as well."

"Aw come on Daddy! I want to know what happens. Can't we at least just call the professor?" Cassie asked as they reached the end of the walkway.

"Cassie, I'm afraid this story is not going to end the way you hope it will. Three years is a long time," Hank said as they got into the car. "In my experience, people don't wait around that long for love."

"May I please see the card?" Cassie asked, as Hank shifted his car into drive.

"Doctor Peter Anderson," read Cassie. "Mom and I will call him, Daddy! You don't have to worry about it."

"I wouldn't get your hopes up, but okay," Hank agreed, handing the letter to her.

Hank stopped at the top of the Eagan driveway, already beginning to think about his upcoming work day.

"OK, thanks, Daddy," she said, kissing him on the cheek and getting out of the car.

"Bye, Sweetie," Hank said as he pulled out his phone to call a co-worker.

As she approached the house, Cassie saw Daniel next to his bike in the garage studying some documents. He quickly stuffed them in his backpack and swung the pack over his shoulders.

"What was that?" Cassie asked as she walked up to him. "Was that the other letter we found?"

"I don't know what you're talking about," Daniel said, annoyed at her prying.

"Don't give me that Danny! Is it addressed to Sarah as well?"

He ignored her. "Did you and Dad make the delivery?" Daniel said as he began walking his bike toward the road.

"She doesn't live there anymore, but we got the name of one of her friends who might know where she is. Hey, where are you going?"

"None of your business!"

"Does Mom know?"

"I'm going to the school to play soccer," Daniel said.

"Where's your soccer ball?" Cassie yelled after him.

"I'm meeting some friends there," Daniel huffed, looking back over his shoulder and yelling as he reached the top of the driveway where his dad was parked, still talking on the phone.

Inside, Buster wagged his tail to welcome Cassie as she rushed passed him on her way to the kitchen to get a snack.

Hearing a commotion outside, she went to the window and noticed Daniel had stopped next to her dad's car door and they were yelling at each other.

"There they go again," she said to Buster, who seemed to only be interested in the cookies she had in her hand.

Cassie gave Buster a chocolate chip cookie and popped one in her mouth. Looking at Peter Anderson's business card, she thought of Jacob and Sarah. She had to try and help them get back together.

She picked up the phone to call Dr. Anderson and when he didn't answer, she left him a message.

Outside, Daniel screamed a parting blow as his dad drove away. He mounted his bike and started weaving up the hill. He didn't notice the old Ford Fairlane parked on the other side of the road. It moved toward him from behind, slowly gaining ground.

The University of South Carolina, Columbia, a little while earlier

Professor Peter Anderson pulled into his parking place at the Physics department at USC.

He hurried up the stairs and swung around the corner into his colleague Jimmy Bouillion's office, where he was waiting.

"Why in the world do you have to schedule meetings so early during summer session, Jimmy?" Peter complained as he plopped down in the chair across the desk from where Jimmy was seated. "One of the main reasons I became a professor was to enjoy leisurely summers."

"It's about time you got here, Doc!" Jimmy chided.

"Sorry," Peter said as he mockingly looked at his watch. "I didn't realize I was three minutes late."

"Anyway, let's get started," Jimmy replied, a bit tersely.

"I have a meeting with Dr. Derrick in a few minutes and I need to get something off my chest." Jimmy said, looking sternly at his mentor.

"About what?"

"About this," Jimmy replied, holding up a bound leather journal.

"The manuscript of my novel?" Peter said.

"You're a horrible liar, Doc." Jimmy said. "My wife told me everything the night before last."

Peter stared at Jimmy, realizing his whole cover up was about to unravel.

"Marlee kept your secret from me pretty well these past few years, but after eliminating everyone else, I realized it had to be you who voted me out of the meteorite project. Marlee came clean and told me everything."

Peter was surprised Jimmy's wife, Marlee, had remembered the details. It was all like a fading dream in his mind. If he hadn't written it all down in the journal Jimmy held in his hand, he was sure little would have been recalled.

"After I figured it out," Jimmy continued, "I've been calling you Brutus. You stabbed me in the back, Doc. She tried to explain you did it to try and save our friendship, but I don't buy it."

Peter said nothing, but looked intently at his longtime friend and colleague. Jimmy was a brilliant scientist and Peter didn't want him to have an opportunity to make the same mistakes he did. When Jimmy discovered his journal a few weeks ago in the lab, calling it a work of fiction was all he could think of.

Peter didn't want anyone else to succumb to the temptations he'd faced a few years earlier. Changing the events of time are not a good idea. You don't realize how even the difficult things you go through form important parts of who you are.

It started with Jimmy's discovered of an element with negative mass during meteorite deposit research. Around the same time Peter developed a devise which could send powerful bursts of light into space. Working together, they realized that the presence of an element with negative mass can keep a black hole open long enough to send pulses of light back in time. And that's exactly what he and Jimmy did using Morse code. Knowing that he was looking at the sky back in 1968, Peter sent a message back to himself to try and prevent his friend's suicide.

But the whole thing went powerfully wrong. Changing an event which has already occurred can affect so many things, including even Peter's marriage. When terrorist got involved and used this technology to try and destroy the United States, their science experiment was becoming a global catastrophe.

The only way Peter could set things back right was to send another message back instructing himself to keep Jimmy from joining the meteorite research team.[1]

The whole story, including the details of how he and Jimmy were able to send light pulses back in time, were in the journal Jimmy now held in his hand.

---

[1] Beyond Time, the prequel to Hope Remains details Jimmy and Peter's adventures in changing the events of time.

FOUR

Jimmy held up Peter's journal. "Now I know this is not fiction."

"But Jimmy, since we were able to get things straightened out, that altered time experience never really happened. It *is* fiction. Please give me my journal." Peter asked, standing up and holding out his hand to retrieve his journal.

"Doc, I'll give it back to you soon. But I want to hold onto it for a little longer."

"Why?"

"I'm meeting with Dr. Derrick in a few minutes," Jimmy said, looking at his watch. "Evidently there's been a new particle discovered during the meteorite research project, a particle with negative mass."

Jimmy looked directly at Peter with a knowing smile.

"Jimmy!" Peter approached him to take back the journal, but Jimmy quickly stuffed it in his brief case and spun the dial to lock it.

"Believe me," Peter warned sternly. "You do not want to make the same mistake I did. Life's events happen for a reason. Don't mess with them! Even the smallest change can affect so much."

"Doc, let me tell you a story," Jimmy said as he pulled a thumb drive from the USB port in his computer. "Back in the 1800s, baths were more of a luxury. In fact, it was common practice to draw a bath for the entire family on a Saturday night."

"What in the world are you talking about?"

Ignoring Peter's interruption and moving toward the door, Jimmy continued, "Families would take baths in eldest to youngest order, starting with the father. With every person, the bath water became dirtier and dirtier. By the time the baby was bathed, it was almost black."

"Jimmy, what does this have to do with anything?" Peter approached him, his anger rising. "You have no right to keep my journal!"

"When they were all done with their baths, the baby was sitting in water so black you had to be careful not to throw the baby out with the bath water."

Jimmy paused for affect and then continued, "Doc, what you are proposing to do is cast away everything that was accomplished because it turned out bad for you. If handled wisely this discovery could be the very key to erasing the pains of the human race. I'd say that's a baby worth saving."

"Jimmy, you have no idea what you're doing!"

Jimmy left the room and Peter heard his footsteps rapidly ascending the steps toward Dr. Derrick's office on the next floor.

Peter hurried to catch up with Jimmy, but it was no use, he heard the door to Dr. Derrick's office close as he was halfway up the stairway.

Still stunned by their conversation, he descended the stairs and stumbled into the increasingly warm South Carolina summer morning.

He slouched down on a bench right outside the door. It was a landscaped area between the Physics department and the Computer Science building. A tranquil spot, with bright flowers and a pleasant aroma of honey-suckle. He often spent time there, sitting in quiet when the 'excitement' of family and career overwhelmed him.

"Not again," he said, as he buried his bald head in his hands.

His cell phone rang but he ignored it. After a few moments, he heard the familiar tone of a new voicemail.

What Jimmy said upset him. He seemed determined to change an event in history and repeat the whole fiasco.

"You okay Peter?"

Peter flinched. Someone had slipped beside him on the bench. It was Alfred, a friend he'd met during the adventure in time he was just talking about with Jimmy.

"Alfred?" said Peter.

"Yes, it's me Peter. You don't look like you're having a very good day."

"You really do exist," Peter exclaimed, ignoring his question.

"Of course I exist. Why did you think I didn't?"

"I couldn't track you down anywhere after we straightened out my interferences with time."

Alfred smiled and laid his hand on Peter's shoulder. "Peter, it's been a rough few years. Shortly after I saw you last, we found out Susan had cancer."

Peter saw the sadness in the elderly black man's eyes. He couldn't help but think of his mom's recent death.

"We moved to Atlanta, seeking the best medical care," Alfred continued. "Had some special times together there for a few years; joined a small fellowship group in the community and made some great friends. Susan died doing what she loved. Up until the last month of her life she was cooking for families in crisis, writing encouraging notes and just loving folks."

"When did she pass away?"

"It's been almost six months now." Alfred Paused. "I miss her every day.

Our friends in Atlanta helped me so much. They surrounded me, loving me the same way Susan had loved them. I didn't feel so alone.

"Susan's death really was like a homecoming. I know she's with Jesus now. I'm sad, but I know she's not. That was my mindset during her funeral and it really was more of a celebration of her life than anything else."

"Homecoming, huh? That's a good way to put it," Peter said. He almost mentioned his mother's death, but realized he was still not ready to talk about it.

"What brings you here if you felt so supported in Atlanta?"

"I've honestly asked myself the same question. Susan and I didn't live here in Columbia long enough to get to know many folks. So, I didn't move back because I know a bunch of people."

"You moved back?"

"Rented an apartment a few blocks from here, near Finlay Park." Alfred pointed in the direction of the park. "I just unpacked the last box yesterday."

Peter asked again, "But why did you leave what you had in Atlanta?"

"Well, Peter, I don't know the full reason yet, but I believe strongly that God directed me back here. I've been trying to discern how to yield to Him, even if it doesn't agree with what I want. I really wanted to stay in Atlanta, but my heart was calling me here. And you're one of the first people I wanted to contact."

"You always seem to show up at a time of need," Peter said. "I was just agonizing over a decision my colleague is making which could lead to the same problems you helped me out of before."

"Well, I'm glad to hear that," Alfred said with a wry smile. "Not that you are agonizing, but that I'm here when you need me."

"Yes, there's a lot to be said for being with a friend during hard times. Just your presence seems to take the edge off. I can't get into it now, but can we talk again soon?"

"Absolutely; Now that I've found you, we'll get together soon. I'm in the Waterford apartments near the park, 101C," Alfred said as he stood up. "I think I'll enjoy a morning walk."

Alfred held his arms open wide and gave Peter a big hug. He then set out toward downtown.

Peter watched Alfred disappear around the corner of the physics building. He was amazed at how settled Alfred seemed, even though he'd just lost his wife. He wondered how someone could get to a place of such peace.

He pulled out his phone and listened to his voice mail. It was from a young girl named Cassie, asking for help in finding Sarah Jenkins.

Sarah Jenkin's brother Ben was the friend Peter had tried to keep from committing suicide by sending his message back in time. The very thing he'd just been discussing with Jimmy.

And then Alfred shows up. This was becoming a very strange day. And it was still morning.

Peter redialed Cassie's number.

FIVE

"Hello," answered the voice of an adult female.

"Hello, ma'am," My name is Dr. Peter Anderson. I got a call from this number from a Cassie. Cassie Eagan."

"Yes, hello Dr. Anderson. I'm Tammy Eagan. Seems my daughter's been quite busy trying to solve the world's problems this morning. I'm sorry she bothered you. When Cassie gets on a mission, she's very tenacious!"

"Tenacity isn't always a bad thing," Peter laughed; "As long as it's for a good cause."

"She certainly thinks it is. Cassie and her brother found an unopened letter in a shack behind our house. Though I assure you they were taught to not open other people's mail, they opened it anyway. It is an apology and an informal proposal from a man named Jacob Younginer to a woman named Sarah Jenkins. Cassie is convinced they're destined to be together. She believes it's up to her to make it happen by getting Jacob's letter to Sarah.

"She and her father tried to deliver it to Sarah this morning. She used to live on Weed Drive, the next street over. But Sarah's moved. The lady who lives there now says you might know where she.

There was a pause, but then Tammy continued. "I'm afraid you're not the only one Cassie's called today,"

Tammy said. "It's amazing how much has happened this morning while I was at work for a few hours."

"What do you mean?"

"She also called Jacob Younginer. She got his number from the letter. He's on his way here from Charleston."

"On his way, huh?" Peter said, feeling in the middle of an unfolding drama.

"Do you know Jacob Younginer?" Tammy asked.

"Sarah mentioned him. She thought he was the one, but all of a sudden she wouldn't talk about him anymore."

"Well, I guess it's really none of our business here at the Eagan household, but somehow we have found ourselves part of a very intriguing story. How often do you find a letter of this magnitude that, for whatever reason, was never delivered?"

Not waiting for an answer, she continued, "So, like it or not, we're in the middle of this story and my daughter can speak of nothing else. She's convinced that Jacob Younginer and your friend Sarah still love each other and her finding the letter is what's going to make it all right."

"Well I do know where Sarah is," Peter said. "But I'm afraid Mr. Younginer isn't going to like what I have to say. Do you mind if I come by and meet Jacob Younginer and tell him where Sarah is in person? I'd at least feel better having met him."

"Why not," Tammy chuckled. "I might as well have two strange men in my house instead of just one."

There was an awkward pause until Tammy said, "I'm partially kidding. Not that you are strange, but I've never met you or Jacob Younginer."

"No, I understand," Peter sympathized. "Is there any way your husband could be there as well?"

"That would make it worse. If we invited Hank, that would make three strange men. He and I have been separated for almost a year."

"Got cha. I'm sorry to hear that," Peter replied, resisting the temptation to ask why and instead changing the subject. "You said Cassie and her brother found the letter. Is your son going to be there?"

"He's at the school soccer field. I expect him home soon."

"Well, I assure you Tammy, if your son has not returned by the time I get there, I will do my best to provide gentlemanly protection for you and Cassie."

"Somehow, I believe you, Dr. Anderson."

"Good. Call me Peter please."

"Okay Peter, thanks."

So, I know where Weed Drive is, what street do you live on and what time do you want me?"

"Jacob Younginer should be here anytime now. So, you can come whenever you'd like."

Tammy then gave Peter their address and they hung up.

Finlay Park, downtown Columbia - around lunch time the same day

Hank Eagan took an early lunch and walked the couple of blocks from his work to fix a sandwich at home. He was sitting on a retaining wall in front of his town house. A soggy tuna fish sandwich hung loosely in his hands as he stared at the waterfall. He didn't seem to notice the gray and white cat enjoying the pieces of tuna that dropped to the pavement ten or twelve feet below.

"How had it happened again?" He asked himself. He didn't want to argue with Daniel anymore, yet it happened every time they saw each other. He just asked him about the other letter he and Cassie had found in the shack. He thought he asked in a kind way. Yet, Daniel was defensive and disrespectful once again.

No matter what he did to try and get close to Daniel, things only seemed to get worse.

He took a bite of his sandwich and turned up his lip in disgust. What a horrible sandwich he'd made! How did Tammy make tuna taste so good? His always tasted so watery.

He tossed the dripping mess to the pavement and the cat pounced on it.

As much as he hated to admit it, he really missed Tammy. With all he'd done wrong as a husband and a father, she seemed to love him anyway.

Sadness gripped him as his thoughts drifted to Cassie, his sunshine. He knew he'd hurt her too. Why couldn't he just go home? Lately, it seemed Tammy had given up on him as well. Had he thrown away his whole family?

"Why did you throw it away?" A voice from right beside him startled him. He turned and saw an elderly black man standing next to the bench.

"Excuse me, what did you say?"

"Why did you throw it away?"

"I didn't say that out loud! How did you know what I was thinking?"

"No," the black man smiled. "Why did you throw your sandwich away?" He pointed below them to what was left of his tuna fish sandwich as the cat finished it off.

"It was a soggy mess," Hank replied. "I'm a horrible cook."

"Making a tuna fish sandwich is hardly cooking," the man replied. "Did you drain the juice?"

"The juice?"

"Yeah, the oil or spring water, whatever it was packaged in. Leave a little in the can after you drain it. Fill a bowl with mayonnaise, dill and sweet relish first, then scoop in the tuna and mix it up."

"You sound like my wife Tammy. How do you know so much about tuna fish sandwiches?" Hank asked, wondering why he was even talking to this stranger.

"Used to watch my wife, Susan, make them. She made the best."

"Made?"

"Susan died a few months ago," the man said, looking down and then straight ahead.

"I'm sorry," Hank answered.

The man nodded, acknowledging Hank's words.

"Why didn't you ask Tammy to make your sandwich for you?"

The question caught Hank off guard and before he could think of a way to avoid the ugly truth, he found himself answering, "Tammy and I are split up and have been for a number of months now."

"I'm sorry," the man answered. "Do you have kids?"

"Yes, we have two: a girl, Cassie and a boy, Daniel. Daniel's the oldest. He's 14 and she's 10."

"Do you miss your family?"

"To be honest," Hank turned and looked up at the man squarely in the eyes, wondering why in the world he was still talking to a complete stranger. "Yes, very much so, but Daniel and I don't get along. We're always at odds and it makes for a horrible home life."

"Why do you think that is?" asked the man. "Do you mind if I sit down."

"No, I don't mind," Hank said, scooting over a bit to make more room and the elderly man eased down and sat.

"I don't think Daniel's forgiven me for my mistakes," continued Hank.

"Do you want him to forgive you for your sake or for his?"

"What do you mean?"

"Do you want Daniel to forgive you so that you'll feel better or so that his wounded heart would be healed?"

"I don't see a difference."

"An unforgiving and bitter heart can become a cancer to the soul. Do you care what this is doing to Daniel? Or do you only care about things being right with him for your sake, so that you can feel successful as a dad? Kids pick up on that kind of stuff."

Hank almost responded in anger at the question, but it struck him in such an odd way, he could only say, "I don't know."

"Have you been forgiven, Hank?"

"Yes, I believe I have been forgiven by Tammy and Cassie, as I told you, but not by Daniel."

"That's not what I mean. Have you been forgiven?"

"How do you know my name?"

"It's written on the badge around your neck."

Hank looked down at the access badge from his work resting on his chest.

"Hank, how can you ever expect others to forgive you if you haven't forgiven yourself?"

"Wait a minute," Hank stood up. "You're talking about religion. Aren't you? Tammy, put you up to this. Nice try, but whatever the answers to my problems are, I'm not going to search for them in some hocus pocus magic faith place. If you want to talk about religion with me, you might as well talk to me about Humpty Dumpty. That's how much credence I give it."

Surprised at how much anger spewed out, Hank was a bit embarrassed and sat back down.

The two sat in silence for a few moments, watching the satiated gray and white cat lying lazily in the June sun next to the steps.

"Tammy did put you up to this, right?" Hank asked again after a few minutes.

"No, Hank. She didn't," the man said. I've never met Tammy or heard of her until you mentioned her."

Hank nodded his head in acknowledgment, looking straight ahead. The man stood up, laid his hand on Hank's shoulder and said, "Hank, I wasn't talking about religion either."

At that the man turned and began to walk away.

"Hey, I didn't get your name?" Hank called after him.

"I'm Alfred," the man answered. "We'll talk again."

Hank watched as the strange man disappeared down the steps that led to the fountain pool.

A little while earlier at the Eagan home in Irmo, SC

Jacob Younginer pulled into the Eagan's driveway and got out of his car. He took a deep breath before using the few shell-shaped steps to walk to the front door.

All he'd been thinking about was Sarah since he left Charleston two hours earlier. He thought she'd refused to forgive him. But now to learn his letter had never been delivered! He didn't know what to think.

Questions and scenarios swirled in his mind. How would Sarah receive his letter of forgiveness, especially three years late? Had absence made her heart grow bitter? Or had she longed for him the way he'd been longing for her? Would she believe the letter was written three years ago? Is there someone else in her life now? After three years he couldn't forget her, no matter how much he tried. Is there a chance she still loved him?

Slowly he climbed the two steps to the Eagan's front porch, but before he could knock, Cassie flung open the door.

"Do you still love Sarah?" Cassie asked.

"Cassie, Cassie," Tammy laid her arm on her daughter's shoulder. "Why don't you start with hello?"

"Are you Jacob Younginer?" Tammy inquired.

"Yes, I am ma'am," Jacob replied extending his hand.

"Cassie's been very anxious to meet you. My name is Tammy Eagan." Tammy shook Jacob's hand.

"Nice to meet you, Tammy."

"How was your trip?"

"Very long; my mind is swirling."

"Come on in, Jacob," Tammy opened the door and led him from the foyer into the kitchen adjacent to the den. "I'm sure it is. May I get you something to drink?"

"Yes, a glass of water would be great."

"So, you still love Sarah?" Cassie asked as she led Jacob into the den.

"To be honest with you, I've tried to forget her," Jacob said as he sat down in a chair next to a brick fire place. "When she never answered my letter or called me, I figured she wanted to forget me."

"What did you do wrong?" Cassie asked.

"Cassie!" Tammy protested as she handed Jacob a glass of ice water. "That's a very personal question. It's none of our business."

"It's OK, Tammy. I don't mind. After all, if Cassie hadn't found my letter, I never would have known Sarah hadn't received it."

Turning toward Cassie, he said. "Sarah and I were in love a few years ago, I would say pretty deeply in love. We discussed marriage, but I'm older than her and have been a bachelor for so long. Selfishly, I wasn't sure I was ready to share my life with anyone. When I told her I needed a little longer to get used to the idea of marriage, she was really hurt. She broke off our relationship."

"Who's Cindy?" Cassie asked.

"Jacob, you don't have to answer that," Tammy offered.

"No, it's OK. Cindy was a co-worker of mine. Two days after Sarah and I broke up, Cindy showed up at my place unannounced. She'd been an annoyance already at work and Sarah was wary of her, maybe even a bit jealous. Foolishly, I let Cindy in and then I couldn't get her to leave.

"Sarah showed up unexpectedly and concluded the worst. She told me she never wanted to see me again."

"What happened to Cindy?" Cassie asked.

"I don't know. I lost track of her when she moved to Nashville last year."

"So, you still want to marry Sarah, even after all this time?" Tammy asked.

"Well, I had pretty much given up on the idea, but I can't get her out of my mind, I guess my heart was still hoping. Then when I got your call this morning and my hopes have been fanned into a flame."

"So, if we can find out where she is, you would still want to deliver the same message to her?" Tammy asked.

"Absolutely! But you said she doesn't live around here anymore, right?"

"That's right," Tammy answered. "Cassie and her dad tried to deliver your letter this morning, but as I mentioned, she's moved.

"But as Cassie told you, we have the name of one of Sarah's friends, a Doctor Anderson. Do you know him?"

"I never met him, but Sarah did mention him. He was good friends with her deceased brother."

"Well, he should be here soon," Tammy smiled. "Cassie called him as well. And he knows were Sarah is."

Jacob could only nod as he was flooded with thoughts of finally being able to share his heart with Sarah.

"May I see the letter?" Jacob asked after a few moments.

Tammy handed it to him. He unfolded it and slowly read through the words he'd written three years earlier.

"I still mean every word," he said, as he folded the letter back into the envelope. "Where's your brother, Cassie? You told me that both of you found my letter."

"Letters," Cassie answered. "Both of us found your letters."

"What do you mean, Cassie?" Tammy asked.

"I didn't tell you about the other letter yet, Mom."

"What other letter? I thought the other letters where just bills," said Tammy.

"There's one other letter Daniel has. He held on to it when I snatched the letters from him yesterday. I saw on the return address that it was from you as well." Cassie confessed, looking over at Jacob.

"Cassie! Why didn't you tell me about the other letter?" Tammy asked sternly.

"I was going to, Mom, but I didn't think it mattered much."

"Who was it addressed to, Cassie? Do you remember?" Jacob asked.

"I didn't see, who." Cassie said. "But I noticed the word Selwood, without a number.

"Selwood?" Jacob repeated, trying to recall what other letter he may have written during that same time.

"Do you remember what other letter it could have been?" Tammy asked.

Jacob's countenance suddenly changed and Tammy picked up on it.

"Jacob, do you remember something?" Tammy asked.

"There was another letter I remember sending. In fact, I mailed it the same day I mailed Sarah's. It was a letter concerning some family business." Jacob stopped there, not wanting to get into any details about the map and letter he found in his grandfather's attic.

"Did you say your brother Daniel has that letter?" Jacob asked Cassie.

"Yes, he tried to hide it from me," Cassie answered.

"I'd really like to get that letter from him as well," Jacob said. "It has an important map in it."

"A map, huh," Tammy replied. "Daniel loves maps."

At that moment the Eagan's dog, Buster, began to bark outside. Tammy went to the window to see who it was.

"I think Peter Anderson is here," she said.

SIX

"This is awesome sweet-tea!" Peter said as he took a sip and sat in the chair next to Jacob. "You should try some, Jacob."

"I would, but I'm a diabetic," Jacob replied, noticeably deep in thought. "I'm sure it's good."

"I have just the thing!" Tammy popped up out of her seat. "Would you like some homemade diet lemonade?"

"That would be great," Jacob smiled.

Soon Tammy appeared with a tall icy glass and handed it to Jacob. He drank three long gulps and wiped his lips with his index finger.

"I don't know if I've witnessed anyone enjoy my lemonade the way you just did," Tammy said, ready with the pitcher to fill Jacob's glass back up.

"This is really good," Jacob said. "It tastes just like real lemonade. As a diabetic, I look for beverages like this I can enjoy without my blood sugar spiking."

"Do you have type 1 or 2?" Tammy asked as she filled another glass with ice from the refrigerator.

"I have a rare type which is classified as 1.5. It's when you get type one, but later in life. They thought I was type 2 until last year.

"How'd you find out?" Peter asked.

"I was really, really thirsty one summer a few years ago. No matter how much water I drank, I needed more. Like cracked red soil, I stayed thirsty. I thought it was just because it was an unusually hot summer, but when my friend suggested that I take my blood sugar it was over 500."

"Over 500!" Tammy said in surprise, as she sat down with her own glass of lemonade. "Have you got it under control now?"

"For the most part," Jacob replied. "I take insulin now. I get some spikes every now and then and sometimes some lows. But as long as I eat well, I'm usually okay."

"I know that can be discouraging," Tammy replied. "My uncle had diabetes and it was a constant struggle."

"Had?"

"Yes, Uncle Ed died a few years ago of complications," Tammy answered, wishing she hadn't brought it up. "But you seem to be taking care of yourself much better than he did."

"I'm trying," Jacob replied, taking another sip of lemonade.

"Do you know where Sarah is?" Cassie asked Peter, tired of the small talk.

"You'll have to excuse my daughter," Tammy responded. "She's a focused young lady."

"Yes she is," Peter laughed. "When I listened to her voice message I was struck by her enthusiasm."

"She's very compassionate," Tammy added, smiling at her daughter and running her hand down the back of her head adjusting her braids. "I know she'll be able to encourage many folks; if she can work on her timing."

"Yes, I do know where she is," Peter answered Cassie. Then he looked over at Jacob.

"Did you ever try and contact her during the past three years?" Peter asked him.

"I hurt her pretty badly," Jacob said. "She told me she never wanted to see me again. When she didn't answer my letter, I figured I had my answer."

"Did you try to visit her?" said Peter.

"Yes, once. I kept thinking time would heal all the pains, hers and mine. But as much as I've tried to move on, I can't imagine my life without her. Sarah is one of those people who is stunningly beautiful on the outside, but even more beautiful on the inside.

"I rang her door bell a couple of months ago, but a lady there told me she had moved."

"Daddy and I met the same lady today," Cassie said. "She said Sarah had a lot of cats."

"Yes, she always has had a soft spot for cats," Peter said. "I've known Sarah since we were kids. She has been through many tragedies.

"I don't know how much she told you about her past," he said, looking at Jacob, "but her inner beauty didn't come without the pruning of great personal suffering. Flowers bloom with the grey skies of spring rain."

"Yes, she told me about her dad, her brother and she told me about her time in the mental hospital. That's what makes it all the more painful," Jacob admitted. "To think that my selfishness added to what she has already been through has been hard to bear."

"Sarah is living at her family place on Kiawah Island," said Peter.

"Where her mom used to live?" Jacob asked.

"Yes, that's the place. Have you been there?" Peter asked, finishing off his tea.

Tammy stood up and grabbed Peter and Jacob's glasses and took them to the kitchen for refills.

"She and I visited there a couple of times when we were together," Jacob answered. Is she with her mom? I know her mom also has a place in Greenville."

"I don't think her mom is down there with her now, but she's not alone. She is with a man and, as far as I know, they are living together."

Jacob tossed his head back hard on the chair he was sitting on and looked up at the ceiling.

"Are they married?" Cassie erupted, standing up.

"No, I don't think so; at least not yet," Peter said. "She's with a guy she met at the hospital."

"The mental hospital?" Jacob asked.

"I'm afraid so," Peter continued. "And as I was telling Tammy, she's been very secretive about the whole thing."

"Did you meet the guy?" Jacob asked.

"Once. His name is Matt and I don't trust him at all. He's not the kind of man I've hoped Sarah would end up with. Ever since she's been with him, she's pulled away from everybody but him. I've been worried about her. In fact, I was telling my wife I was thinking about driving down there to make sure she's okay. I know that would be prying, but she's like my little sister. Her brother and I were best friends."

Jacob grabbed his letter to Sarah from the coffee table and stuffed it back in the envelope and stood up.

"I'm going to deliver my letter to Sarah," he said with resolve. "She needs to know how I feel. Even if she ends up marrying this Matt guy, I want to let her know how much I still love her."

"Yes!" Cassie stood up cheering. "Will you let us know what she says?"

"Absolutely. Thank you so much for contacting me. I'll call you guys and let you know how it turns out."

When Peter stood up to shake his hand goodbye, Jacob said, "Dr. Anderson, can you walk outside with me. I want to make sure I remember where her condo is?"

Jacob said his goodbyes to Tammy and Cassie and Peter followed him out to his car.

"Call me Peter," he said as they walked up the driveway.

"Okay," Jacob said, turning and facing him.

"Peter, I just found out a few minutes ago that the Eagan kids found a second letter of mine which wasn't delivered."

"Was it also to Sarah?"

"No, it's a long story, but it's a family letter, with a map of some graves."

"Graves?"

"Yes, not too far from here, over by the high school in the river bed of Hollenshed Creek, near where it flows into the Broad River."

"Do you mean Hope Creek?" Peter asked. "I know that area. I've fished the Broad near there."

"Some people do call that part of Hollenshed, Hope Creek and there's a reason for it.

"The bodies buried in that grave yard all died during the same year, 1749 and they all have the same last name: Hope. No one knows how all these people died, but my letter has information which may shed some light on the mystery.

"I don't want to get into the details now, but do you have time to wait around until their son, Daniel returns and get the letter from him? You can either get it back to me, or deliver it to Dr. Shuler. The letter's addressed to him. I didn't want to say too much about it to Tammy. It's not a very pleasant subject."

"Sure. I can do that," Peter said.

"There should be three documents in the envelope: a letter from me to Dr. Shuler, the map to the graves and a short letter from my Uncle Luke."

Jacob handed Peter his business card with his phone number. "Call me when you get the letter from the boy."

"Okay I will," Peter said, pulling a card from his wallet and giving it to Jacob. "And you call me once you've delivered your letter to Sarah. Let me know how she is."

"Will do," Jacob replied.

A little while later at Hank's office

"What's wrong?" Hank asked as he answered his cell phone and slipped out of his cubicle. He walked over to the window next to the conference room to have a bit of privacy.

Lately, anytime he got a call from Tammy there was some kind of emergency.

"When did you last see Daniel?" Tammy asked sternly.

"I saw him this morning. He said he was heading out to the soccer field at school."

"Did you know about the other letter from Jacob Younginer?"

"Cassie told me he had another letter, but when I asked him about it we got into another argument. He started in with me again in angry tones right off the bat. We ended up in our usual shouting match."

"Hank, one of these days you're going to have to stop thinking so much about how hurt you feel and realize how hurt your son is. Have you ever really considered that? Daniel's anger comes from some really deep hurt."

"Don't you think I get that by now? I know you think I'm a horrible dad, but I still love my kids; both of them, believe it or not."

Hank was speaking louder than he realized and several co-workers raised their heads over the cubicle walls to see what the commotion was.

"Hank, once again, this is not about you. I'm starting to worry about Daniel. He hasn't come home since you saw him."

"Tammy, it's not even 5'oclock yet. I'm sure he'll show up soon. You need to stop babying him."

"Sorry to bother you, Hank." Tammy hung up.

SEVEN

Almost half past 5 that same afternoon on I-26 East toward Charleston

As Jacob approached the exit to Highway 17 South off of Interstate 26, it struck him that he'd been on this same road going the opposite direction earlier that day. It was ironic to him that he spent all this time thinking about Sarah and she was only a few miles away from him on Kiawah Island.

Jacob tried to imagine what the man Sarah was living with was like. Peter said his name was Matt and that he didn't trust him. This worried Jacob. As much as he longed to be with Sarah the rest of his life, there was an equal, if not stronger desire that she end up safe and happy, regardless.

Jacob had every intention of taking this guy Matt out if he even looked at Sarah wrong.

As he passed the turn off for James Island, Jacob continued on Highway 17 toward Kiawah. Then it occurred to him that Kiawah is a secured island. He couldn't get in without a pass.

Jacob tapped his blue tooth and used voice activation to call Michael Romo, a golf buddy who sold real estate on the island. When Michael didn't pick up, he left a message.

"Hey Michael, this is Jacob. Looking forward to golf on Tuesday. I should be able to meet you by four thirty. Listen, I need a favor. Can you call in a pass for me at the Kiawah security gate? I need to take care of something there. Thanks. Call me if that's a problem."

Jacob tapped his blue tooth again to end the call and turned onto the long section of shaded road leading to the entrance of Kiawah Island. It was his favorite stretch of pavement on the planet. The beauty of the majestic oaks yielding their swaying gray garland invited you to the hidden beauty of the island's forest beaches.

His thoughts drifted back to Sarah. He remembered the night of passion in the dunes near her mom's place on Kiawah Island before they broke up. Up until then, she'd insisted their relationship remain pure. She'd given her love to him and he'd selfishly, cowardly tossed it aside. If he only knew then how he felt now.

Anxiety rose. He could barely breathe. Soon he would see her and could tell her how much he loved her. He planned to ask her on bended knee to be his wife. He didn't care if this Matt guy was standing right there. Sarah had to know how he felt about her.

Then he thought of how hurt Sarah was the last night he saw her. Cindy seemed to have been waiting for a chance to pounce in. He should have seen through her schemes.

Before he knew it, it was late into the night and she was half drunk on his wine. Sarah could not have picked a worse moment to pop in. What was she still doing in town? She knocked on the door and then peered into the living room. Cindy had just leaned into him on the couch and he was moving away from her drunken advances. But it was 1:30 in the morning. From all appearances, Cindy was spending the night with him and he was snuggling with her on the couch.

Why did he ever let Cindy in? Why didn't he make her leave much earlier? It all seemed so much like a set up. Had Cindy somehow contacted Sarah and bragged that she was with him?

These were all questions he'd been asking over and over again the last three years.

Jacob pulled up to the security gate at Kiawah and asked if Michael Romo had left a pass for Jacob Younginer.

"Nothing here for you, Mr. Younginer," the guard replied, after flipping through the passes on her desk. "If you want to try contacting him again, you can back up and pull over to the right in front of the chain linked fence."

Jacob nodded and tried to produce a polite smile. As he maneuvered his car to where the guard had instructed him, he redialed Michael's number.

This time Michael answered and arranged for a realty pass. Jacob picked it up and displayed it on his dash board. Soon he was driving past beautifully landscaped golf courses, wooded bike paths and lush meadows leading to the East Beach Resort Center.

It'd been a few years since he'd been to Kiawah, but as he took a right on Sea Forest Drive, memories of his times with Sarah and her mom flooded his mind. He remembered exactly where the Villa was. He turned left on Mariner's Watch.

He could feel his heart pounding. He felt as if he was in a fight for his life. He was never in the military, but he wondered if soldiers in the midst of combat felt as tense as he did.

Sarah's place was at the end of Mariner's Watch, around the corner from a forest path that led right to the beach. As he slowed, he could see a dark grey Lexus parked in front of the Villa. He parked to the right, behind a large oak tree flanked by sea oats. He could look almost directly up the stairs to the villa from that spot, but his car was not in plain sight.

He closed his eyes a moment, pondering his next step. When he opened them, his heart almost stopped. There she was, like an angel appearing out of the shadows of the door way, descending the steps. As she neared the sidewalk at the end of the steps, walking closer and closer to his concealed hideaway behind the oak, he could see her eyes. Nothing could conceal her beauty, but she looked empty and sad. He'd never seen her that way before. It alarmed him. Was she alone? Should he run to her now?

He reached for the letter, but then the villa door opened again.

A tall thin man emerged, talking on a cell phone. He had dark, wavy hair and a scraggly beard, uncut under his chin with bare patches across his cheeks. He was obviously angry with whomever he was talking to. Jacob could hear him yelling as he waved his arms. After a moment, he cried out for Sarah to wait on him as she continued down the sidewalk toward the path to the beach. The man hung up his phone and jogged after her. When he reached her, he grabbed her arm roughly, but she didn't resist.

At that, Jacob eased the car door open and slid out just as the couple disappeared around the corner of the villas toward the beach.

A little earlier in Columbia, SC

Bubba looked over at Daniel, his hands duct taped behind his back and his legs tied with rope. He was only a few feet from the floor planks he had shattered to retrieve Jacob's letters the day before.

"I bet you wish you never stole those letters from me," Bubba said as he pulled another piece of fried chicken from the greasy cardboard barrel. He was on his second six pack of the day by now and was relaxing all inhibitions.

"They weren't your letters anyway!" Daniel raised his voice. "Why did you steal them?"

"None of your business," Bubba said, taking a huge bite of another chicken breast. "I know you have those letters, where are they? If you give them to me I'll let you go. What were you doing down by the river anyway?"

"You have no idea what was in those letters, do you?" Daniel asked, not expecting an answer. Though he was being held against his will, Bubba didn't frighten him. As mean and fierce as he tried to act, Bubba had some real problems. Daniel actually felt a little sorry for him.

"Who told you to steal them?" Daniel asked, feeling surprisingly brave considering his circumstances.

"Maybe I just wanted them," Bubba said as he took another crunchy bite of a thick thigh and ignored the chicken grease rolling down his cheek and neck.

"Your parents are probably beginning to worry about you by now. It's getting late," Bubba said, beginning to slur his words. "Where are the letters?"

"I told you I don't have them," Daniel said.

As Bubba drank more beer and finished off the box of chicken, he regretted he'd called MB the night before. He was afraid he would somehow find out anyway and he didn't want to incur his crazed wrath.

Now he realized that if he hadn't told MB about the letters being stolen, he may have never found out. But now that MB knows, he had to get them back.

"Where are the letters?" Bubba yelled again, now starting to wonder what he was going to do if Daniel didn't tell him soon.

In the meantime, Daniel was contemplating telling Bubba where he'd stuffed the map and the two letters. That morning, he was able to slide the documents under a moss-covered rock even as Bubba grabbed him. He almost got away. However, the river on one side and a rock face on another prevented him from escaping Bubba's grasp.

Bubba drug him back to his car parked along the dirt road and threw him in the front seat next to a bucket of chicken.

Back at the cabin, Daniel noticed Bubba was starting to doze off. He slowly loosened the trappings around his leg. When his legs were almost free, Bubba's phone rang. He reached down and grabbed it from a pile of newspapers on the dusty floor.

"Hello?"

"Did you get the letters?" asked an irritated MB.

"I have the boy and I'm trying to find out where he hid them?"

"You idiot! Why would you kidnap a boy? What are you going to do with him?"

"I didn't kidnap him. I'm going to get the letters from him, MB!"

"Don't say my name! He had better not be there with you while you're saying that."

"Of course not," Bubba lied as he scrambled to his feet and began wrestling with the decayed front door of the old cabin in the woods behind his mother's house.

"Bubba, you have a real problem on your hands. You kidnapped a boy and the police are going to hunt you down. Get those letters back and you better never mention my name!"

Bubba could hear MB yelling at someone as the call went dead. He was horrified in spite of his intoxication. He had to get those letters and do something with the boy.

He squeezed back into the front door he had only partially opened a few moments ago, but to his dismay, Daniel was gone.

EIGHT

Daniel dropped from the screen-less window into a thicket of ivy and small oak tree sprouts moments before Bubba re-emerged from the porch after talking with MB. Daniel's hands were still taped and his legs partially bound. Already he could hear Bubba bounding down the decaying front steps in his pursuit.

Daniel looked around and made a split-second decision to roll under the dark crawl space below the cabin. He managed to maneuver into the shadows, but he gained a mouthful of spider web. He also heard the rustling of a creature retreating to the center of the musty hide away. Bubba hurried down the steps and cleared the thick bush around the old cabin. Looking down the hill toward the creek he saw no sign of Daniel. Figuring his prisoner had escaped out the window, Bubba circled around the right of the porch, getting tangled in a patch of ivy and toppling over face down. He was 20 feet from where Daniel had dropped from the cabin window.

Daniel could see his kidnapper from the veiled darkness. He dared not make a sound. His heart was beating rapidly and he tried to keep his breathing shallow.

Bubba didn't move for a few moments. Then he slowly tried to roll his rotund body to his knees to get up. Even that little bit of exertion winded him. He straightened his arms and raised his knees towards his belly, but then collapsed with a bounce.

As Daniel lay breathless, he heard the movement under the shack again, this time coming toward him. He remained motionless, but then a creature passed through a slice of afternoon sun and he saw it, letting out a muffled yell in surprise.

Back on Kiawah Island, Costal South Carolina

Jacob got out of his car and following Sarah and the man from a safe distance. When he reached the boardwalk, he could see the couple turn left, walking east toward the Sanctuary Inn in the middle of the island. He walked swiftly back to his car and formulated a plan. He drove to the Sanctuary parking lot, parked his car and jogged on the meticulously manicured stone walkway down to the beach.

When he got to the sand he kicked off his socks and shoes and shielded his eyes from the afternoon sun, peering toward the west end of the island. Looking along the beach as the low tide waters lapped lazily across the sand, he saw a man on a bicycle approaching rapidly.

Then, looking more toward the middle of the beach, he could see Sarah and the man she was with walking toward him. They were about 300 yards down the beach between the rhythmic water line and the sea oat dunes, which were flanked by the boardwalks leading from the hotels and villas.

Jacob decided to continue along the wave line. The coolness of the sea water rushing over his toes and the smell of the salty fresh surf calmed him momentarily. He closed his eyes and took a deep breath, trying to settle his soul. He felt for the letter in his pocket. Sarah would soon know how he felt about her.

He had to tell her. No matter what the circumstances, no matter what could have happened in her life these last three years, he still felt the same way. He could not escape his love for Sarah Jenkins.

His hands trembled as the distance between them lessened. When he was so close he could see the emotionless stare on Sarah's face, he began angling to the middle of the beach. When their eyes met, he could tell she didn't recognize him or maybe she couldn't comprehend it could be him.

But then she knew! Her eyes grew wide and her mouth hung open. Perhaps there was a hint of hope in her eyes, but he wasn't sure.

As Jacob approached them, the man pulled Sarah behind him and assumed a defensive posture.

"Jacob!" Sarah yelled as the man moved toward him.

What happened next was so bizarre, Jacob's mind could hardly take it. He saw each detail in such striking clarity that it seemed to happen in slow motion. In the moments before he blacked out, the pained expression on Sarah's face etched in his mind. Sarah didn't want to be with the man she was with. He knew it.

She reached out her arms to keep the man from Jacob and yelled, "Matt, don't hurt him!"

Matt brushed her aside and charged toward Jacob. The look on his face was not just determined, but intensely angry. Jacob saw a gun and felt the force of the blow above his right ear. His body fell helplessly in a mound upon the sand.

Earlier at the Eagan's house in Irmo, SC

"How long will it take for Jacob to get to where Sarah is?" Cassie asked, as she crashed into the kitchen where Tammy and Peter were talking about Daniel.

"It's about a two-and-a-half-hour drive from here," Peter replied.

"Is he going to let us know what Sarah says?"

"I'm sure we'll find out, honey," said Tammy. "But I'm concerned about your brother now. He should've been home hours ago."

Peter was pondering whether to bring up what Jacob told him about the map, when they heard the front door opening.

"Daniel," Tammy cried out, but then her hopes were dashed. As she hurried into the foyer, she saw her estranged husband.

"Hank, I've asked you to knock," She complained. "I thought you were Daniel."

"He's still not here?"

"No! And it's after five," Tammy replied in a slightly high-pitched tone, as Hank followed her into the kitchen where Peter and Cassie were seated at the table.

Until then Tammy had been able to remain outwardly calm. However, the inner turmoil of her son not returning from a morning bike ride and now Hank being there was beginning to show. Though her love for Hank had not completely died, his self-centered insensitivity kept her from wanting to be around him.

Peter stood up as Hank entered the kitchen and extended his hand, "Hey, Mr. Eagan. I'm Peter Anderson."

"This is Sarah's friend," Cassie announced. "The one the lady told us about this morning."

"Yes, I remember the name," Hank returned the hand shake. "Were you able to help locate Sarah Jenkins?"

"Yes, as a matter of fact, Jacob Younginer is delivering his letter to her personally on Kiawah Island as we speak." Peter answered.

"That'll be interesting," Hank responded.

"What did you say you were arguing about with Daniel this morning, Hank?" Tammy asked, her tone turning sharp.

"I told you!" Hank replied, instantly feeling defensive. "I was asking him if he had another letter from Jacob Younginer."

"What did he say?" Peter asked.

"He said no," Hank said, turning toward Peter, surprised that he would jump in the middle of his family discussion.

Understanding the awkwardness, Peter continued. "Before Jacob left he told about the second letter. He mailed it the same day. It contains some family documents and he would like to get it back. He asked me to get it from Daniel when he returns."

"Did he say anything else?" Hank asked.

"He said the letter contained a map to a grave site near the high school."

"Daniel claimed to be playing soccer near the high school," Tammy gasped. "I bet he's out following the map."

At that moment Peter's cell phone rang. He looked and saw who it was.

"Excuse me folks," he said, stepping toward the foyer. "I need to take this call. I'll be back."

It was Jimmy.

NINE

"Hello," Peter said, as he stepped out onto the Eagan's porch and into the heat of the southern afternoon.

"Doc, I'm still mad at you. But I wanted you to know the meeting went even better than I thought it would," Jimmy said.

"Dr. Derrick has given us clearance to repeat the experiment you wrote about in your journal. We're close to really being able to help folks."

"What do you mean help folks, Jimmy?"

"Doc, before you get to ranting again, an old friend of yours wants to talk to you. He was at our meeting today and is joining our efforts. You remember him, Stephen Davis."

"Stephen Davis!" Peter replied. "I thought he was in Wilmington."

"Not anymore."

"You guys are bringing in the big guns on this thing, Jimmy," Peter said. "I.."

"Peter," Stephen interrupted, now on the other end of the phone. "How are you?"

"I'm doing fairly well. It's been a very interesting day," Peter answered, not wanting to say more.

How are the twins?"

"They're good," Peter replied. "They're starting pre-school soon and are bundles of energy. I see why the norm is to have kids when you're a little bit younger. I'm having a blast with them though."

"And Elizabeth, your lovely bride?"

"She and the twins are away for the weekend for a family birthday party. But she's doing fine," Peter answered. "What brings you to your old stomping grounds?"

"Jean and I moved near Charleston, on Kiawah Island, to be closer to my folks. They're getting along in age. I wanted to leave the research field for a while. However, when Jimmy told me about your journal, I read it. Those events had all but faded from my memory. But as I read your account of the events, the memories became clearer.

"We're close to being able to change a past event again, Peter. And I assure you, we'll learn from the mistakes of the first attempt."

"Hold on, Stephen," Peter said, tensely. "I'm not in on this you know. If Jimmy told you I was, that was only wishful thinking."

"Peter, you're the one who developed the Electro Magnetic Spectrometer. Sending pulses of light back in time could never have happened without it."

"I didn't develop it for that," Peter said. "At least that's not what it should be used for now. I thought, like me, you would see how dangerous this kind of process can be. Don't you remember how you got sucked in?"

"Yes I do, Peter. But I want you to listen to my thoughts for a moment."

"Okay. I'll listen, but I have to get off the phone in a couple of minutes. I'm kind of in the middle of something."

"Okay," said Stephen, "I'll make it quick. The way I see it, your first attempt was a recipe for disaster. Going all the way back to 1968 was too far in the past. Change an event that far back and it was bound to have a larger impact, as the ripples of time traveled over decades. No wonder your life ended up so different. This time we need to pick a past event that just happened, before too many changes can occur."

Peter said nothing so Davis continued, "Let's think about this the way heart transplants evolved in the medical field. By scientific advancements, we're now able to allow folks to live longer. In a sense, isn't than the same thing?

"The folks would have died, but we have the technology to save them. Should we let them die because we would be, as you put it, 'playing God'?"

Peter started to respond, but Stephen Davis continued. "Do you really think we are messing in God's arena? Wasn't it God who gave us the wisdom and knowledge to do this in the first place? If done right, this has the potential for saving more lives than heart transplants ever did."

Stephen paused and then continued.

"Peter. Believe me, if anyone knows the danger of this kind of thing as much as you, it's me. Like I said a moment ago, if we're able to try this again, it will be for a much shorter time with great consideration to the affect it will have."

"I must say, Stephen," Peter said, noticing Buster, the Eagan's sheepdog, lumbering across the lawn and taking a dump. "You have thought this thing out and you make some great points."

"So you'll help us? Stephen replied, a bit excited. "We still need to figure out how you were able to fine tune the Morse code blasts to a particular location in time and space."

"No Stephen. I'm not going to help. I can't. As safe as you are trying to make it sound, you'll be getting in way over your heads if you get this working again. Changing a life event is not a good idea, no matter what. It's like you and Jimmy and, whoever else is involved, are trying to harness a tornado. It's way too dangerous. I'm sorry, but I can't be a part of it."

"I'm sorry too, Peter," Stephen answered, in a much more subdued tone than Peter expected. "It's been nice talking with you. I'll be back and forth between here and home for a while. I'm sure I'll see you. Take care."

"You too Stephen."

Peter hung up the phone and stared ahead at the woods across the street from the Eagan home. Stephen made some good points and seemed much more level headed than Jimmy, but the whole thing left him with a feeling of impending doom.

What an unbelievable day this had turned out to be, he thought, as he stepped back into the Eagan house. He was glad Elizabeth and the twins were out of town. He needed some time alone to sort through all that was going on.

"Is everything okay, Dr. Anderson?" Cassie asked, as she noticed him enter the room.

"I hope so," Peter replied, walking over to where Tammy, Hank and Cassie were sitting in the kitchen. "Still no word from Daniel?"

"Not yet," Hank replied, grabbing his keys from the table. "I think I'm going to ride out to the soccer field and see what's going on. Maybe he just got into a game and time got away from him."

"That's a great idea, Peter replied. "I need to head back to my side of town for a while."

"Hank, do you want me to go too?" Tammy asked following Peter and Hank through the foyer.

"No, you stay here with Cassie," Hank said, looking Tammy directly in her eyes. "Hopefully, I'll find him, put his bike in my trunk and we'll be back soon."

Peter and Hank walked out into the front yard together.

"Hank," Peter said. "I told Jacob I would either secure the letter Daniel has or deliver it to the address on the letter. Will you take care of that for me?"

"Yes. I'll do that." Hank responded.

"Thank you. I sure hope you find your boy soon."

"Me too." Hank shook Peter's hand.

They walked to their cars and Tammy watched them drive off in the same direction toward highway 6, she reached down and grabbed Cassie's hand. For the first time in years she felt on the same page with Hank concerning the kids. He actually took initiative and displayed the kind of leadership she'd longed for.

"Do you think Daddy will find Daniel?" Cassie asked.

"I hope so Sweetie."

As Peter hit the highway and merged in with the traffic headed downtown, he rehearsed in his mind where Alfred said he was living. Waterford Apartments 101 C, he remembered. He hated to leave the Eagans in the midst of their search, but with Hank there, he felt he should let him take the lead.

He expected Jacob to call soon with news concerning his search for Sarah. In the meantime, he really wanted to talk to Alfred.

He took the Huger Street exit toward Finlay Park.

In the meantime, Hank saw no sign of any soccer going on at the high school. He searched surrounding the field with no results.

As he turned onto his street, headed back to the house, he wondered if it was time to call the police.

In the woods behind the Eagan's House

Daniel's muffled yell from under the shack, alerted Bubba to his whereabouts. He labored to get to his feet.

Under the shack, Daniel found himself half a foot from a curious approaching possum. Daniel had always been told to flee from possums or raccoons seen during the day, they were probably rabid. As the possum approached, Daniel rolled from under the shack and emerged under the window he had dropped from a few minutes earlier.

He screamed loudly as he scrambled to his feet and came face to face with Bubba who grabbed him in a bear hug and began dragging him back to the shack.

"That won't happen again," Bubba said. "You won't be leaving this shack until you tell me were those letters are. This time I'm going to chain you."

Daniel continued to scream until Bubba covered his mouth with his sweaty hand. Daniel could barely breathe.

Moments before Daniel saw the possum, Hank pulled back into the Eagan drive. When he got out of the car, he noticed Buster barking at the side of the house facing the woods.

"What you barking at boy?" Hank said as he walked toward Buster. Then he heard something faint but distinct coming from the woods. He paused and then heard it again.

TEN

When Bubba drug Daniel back into the cabin, he bound him with more tape and rope and this time he gagged him. Then, after reaching for another beer and finding he had drunk them all, he leaned against the front wall and slid down to the floor.

As the alcohol wore off the reality of what Bubba faced began to sink in. Even if Daniel told him where the letters were, what was he going to do with him? Every angle he ran in his muddled mind came up the same. He was screwed.

Bound tightly and lying face down with his head away from the door, Daniel could hear Bubba struggle to his feet and leave the shack to fetch more beer.

Downtown Columbia

Alfred opened his condo door to find Peter standing there.

"Hey, bet you didn't expect me to track you down this early," Peter said, as Alfred stood aside and motioned for him to come in.

"Welcome to my humble abode, Peter."

"Nice place," Peter said as he entered a sunroom and sat down in the seat Alfred offered him. There was a clear view of the Columbia skyline and the Finlay Park fountain.

"It's all I need," Alfred smiled. "But, I'm afraid it lacks the feeling of home Susan would have added. I'll need to hang up at least a picture or two before long. Can I get you something to drink? I've got water, sweet tea, or sodas."

"Sweet tea sounds fine, thanks." Peter answered, resting his head back and trying to relax.

"What's your day been like?" Alfred asked, as he laid the glass of tea beside Peter. "You look totally exhausted."

"You wouldn't believe what's happened since I saw you this morning."

"Try me," Alfred said.

As the sun dipped lower and lower in the skyline and long shadows chased the day, Peter told him about his phone call from Cassie, his time with the Eagan family, as well as the strange letters from Jacob Younginer.

"And the reason I got involved in the first place," Peter went on; "Was that one of Jacob's letters was a proposal to Sarah. But she never got it and now she's in Charleston with a creepy dude. From where I sit, this Matt guy she's with offers her nothing but pain. She's been through enough pain, Alfred. You know."

"Yes, Peter. I know about what she's been through and I know how protective you are of her because she's your dead friend's sister."

"Then I heard from Jimmy again," Peter continued. "He's got Stephen Davis working on the project now. Remember he's the one who was using our time changing technology for evil before he came to his senses. It sounds like he and Jimmy are close to being able to repeat what we did. And there's no reason to believe the results would be any better."

"Peter, it sounds like you've enough to worry about with trying to help the Eagan family and Sarah. Why are you so anxious about what Jimmy and Stephen are doing?"

"I guess because I feel responsible. I'm the one who conceived the whole time 'travel' scheme in the first place."

"Peter, from what you've told me, you've done all you can to prevent a repeat of what happened a few years ago. Is there anything else you could do?"

"Not really," Peter replied. "I guess I could head over to the lab and try and take my journal back by force. And that wouldn't be a good idea. Jimmy is younger than me and I think much quicker. He was once a pro baseball prospect before he blew out his arm. Other than that, I think I've done all the warning and discouraging I know how to do."

"Okay good," Alfred said, as he took a sip of water and looked out over the skyline at the setting sun. "Have you talked to God about it, asking for him to guide you in your adventure?"

"Well, yes. As I was driving over to the Eagans earlier, but would you really call it an adventure? It seems more like a tragedy."

"Peter, if you've presented the situation to God, asked for His wisdom and committed the outcome to His sovereign control, then it is an adventure. Stop long enough to ask and listen before you proceed. Be sure you're in the role He wants you in and be careful not to force what you want."

Peter took a sip of his tea and stared out the window in thought.

"There is a life verse I want to share with you, Peter."

"A life verse?"

"Yea, a verse so powerful that it can actually guide your life. I call these verses my life GPS."

"Okay, I'm hooked," Peter said, looking over at Alfred and taking another swallow of tea. "What are they?"

"'Trust in the Lord with all your heart and lean not on your own understanding. In all your ways acknowledge him and he will make your paths straight.' Proverbs 3:5-6.

Peter, what these verses are telling you is to set aside your understanding of what Jimmy and his colleagues are doing and trust God in it. Remember His ways are higher than yours. He sees from an eternal perspective. You don't."

Alfred paused for a moment, but when Peter didn't respond, he continued. "Think about the good that came out of the last time you sent those Morse code messages back in time. Your marriage to Elizabeth is much better now because you've realized how thankful you are for her. Another positive is that you and I met."

"That's true," Peter said. "I never really thought about that part of it. In the end, God did use the whole thing to accomplish some powerful connections and reconciliation."

"Exactly," Alfred agreed. "If you think about it, God's Kingdom is about relationships. He's always working at reconciliation, primarily reconciling men and women to Himself. Don't forget how your faith was cemented as a result of what happened."

"Very true," Peter said. "So what you're saying is that I can be at peace about what Jimmy and Stephen are doing; that in spite of my understanding and the way I see the situation, I should fully trust that it's not a surprise to God."

Peter's countenance noticeably changed as he talked.

"I think you're getting it," Alfred said. "Certainly, we're called to do things, but when we have done all we know to do, we trust; not in our understanding, but in God's sovereign reign."

"The way I looked at it what we did, since we're actually changing life's events, is we're playing God', trying to fix one of His mistakes," said Peter.

"Peter, just like God gives a surgeon the wisdom and skills to save a life, He gives scientists like you the abilities to do extraordinary feats. What you and Jimmy did is no surprise to him."

As Peter sat in the beauty of a magnificent sunset, the truth of what Alfred said washed through him like a rushing river. Anxiety and fear were swept away and peace remained.

After a few minutes Peter's cell phone rang. He pulled it out and noticing it was Tammy.

"Hello."

A little while earlier in the woods behind the Eagan's House

Daniel's attempts to free himself were useless. After a while, he heard steps on the porch again and the door open slowly. Bubba must have returned.

Daniel could tell Bubba was getting more and more desperate and it scared him. He planned on telling him where he had hidden the map and the letter from Jacob

Younginer. This whole thing was getting out of hand. He just hoped Bubba would let him go when he told him.

Then the tape was slowly being pulled from his mouth and he could feel his tied hands being freed. Next the bandana was removed from his eyes, he turned and saw it wasn't Bubba. It was his dad.

Hank motioned with a finger to his lips for him to be quiet. He then helped Daniel out the door and down the rickety steps.

"Are you hurt?" Hank whispered as they began the descent down to the creek. Daniel shook his head.

When they made it down to the creek, Hank cut off the rest of the tape and rope Bubba had reinforced.

"Who did this to you?" Hank asked, as he and Daniel moved quickly along the creek toward the bridge that led to their back yard.

Daniel gave him a short summary of what he'd been through since being grabbed at Hollenshed Creek near the high school.

"So there was another letter?" Hank replied, trying not to sound accusatory, but realizing he did anyway.

Daniel said little else as they crossed the bridge and entered the house to Tammy and Cassie's screaming excitement.

Hank called the Lexington Sheriff's Office and told them about Daniel's kidnapping. They agreed to send a deputy right over.

"I don't want to talk to anybody about what happened, Dad," Daniel said tersely when Hank hung up the phone.

Hank could feel hot emotion rushing up his spine. This is what made it impossible for him. Yes, he messed up. He'd been an absent dad, over engrossed in his job. But he was sorry. He wanted to make it right, but what ever he did to make peace was never good enough.

However, Hank didn't say what was on his heart. He bit his lip and said nothing. This was a victory.

He caught what he thought was a sympathetic, appreciative glance from Tammy as she said, "Daniel, honey, we have to call the sheriff's office. Even though the guy wasn't there when your dad rescued you, it doesn't mean he won't come back. He must've followed you out to the high school. So he knows where we live."

"I'm scared!" Cassie announced with a quiver. "If it's the same guy who chased us, he's really big."

"And fat," Daniel sneered.

"Don't worry, sweetie," Hank said, walking over and giving Cassie a hug. "When the deputy gets here, I'm sure he'll track the guy down."

"Can you stay with us tonight, Daddy?"

Hank looked at Tammy as if to see if she was okay with it. She nodded and Hank said. "Okay. I'll stay."

"I'll sleep in the guest bedroom," Hank whispered as he walked over to where Tammy was dialing a number from a piece of paper.

"Hello", Peter said as he answered the phone.

"Peter, this is Tammy Eagan. "Daniel is safe at home!"

"Thank God!" Peter exclaimed.

"I have been thanking Him," Tammy said. "Daniel was kidnapped, but he wasn't hurt. Hank heard him screaming in the woods and found him tied up in the same shack where he and Cassie found the letters."

"Is he okay?"

"Yes, the guy was rough with him, but he's not hurt. A sheriff's deputy is on the way."

"Very good," Peter replied. "Have you heard anything from Jacob Younginer?"

"No, but Cassie asks me every fifteen minutes."

"Hopefully, one of us will hear from him soon," Peter replied. "Hey, any word about the other letter from Jacob?"

"Yes, Daniel did have it. He said he hid it before he was kidnapped."

"Interesting; I'll drive over tomorrow morning and check on things." said Peter.

"That sounds good. We'll be expecting you," Tammy replied.

Early evening, Kiawah Island, SC

"Do you think he'll be okay?" asked the jogger who noticed Jacob hidden in the dunes near the Sanctuary board walk. He was unconscious and still oozing blood from his head.

"I'm not sure, ma'am," answered the paramedic as he and his partner slide Jacob into the back of the ambulance. He's lost a lot of blood. So you didn't see a wallet lying around?"

"No, I sure didn't."

"We're flying blind here. Don't know if he's allergic to anything. Heck, I don't even know who he is. All I know is somebody doesn't like him very much," the paramedic said as he quickly closed the ambulance door as his partner turned on the lights.

ELEVEN

Sirens blaring, the ambulance carrying Jacob Younginer turned onto Calhoun Street and into the Emergency entrance to Charleston Memorial hospital.

Because of the seriousness of his injury, the ambulance was greeted by a medical team ready to transport him to surgery.

"We have a John Doe here," the paramedic said as they lifted Jacob out of the ambulance, making sure to keep his head steady. "No wallet or cell phone. Looks like a robbery. He took a vicious blow to the head."

"We need to get him stabilized," a PA said, as they wheeled him inside.

Alfred's apartment, downtown Columbia

"They found Daniel!" Peter said as he reentered the sunroom after talking to Tammy.

"Excellent. Is he okay?" Alfred asked.

"I think so. He was kidnapped and tied up in the same old shack where he and his sister found Jacob Younginer's letters. Hank, his dad, heard him screaming and set him free."

"That's really good," Alfred responded. "Have they caught the kidnappers?"

"Not yet, but Tammy said the sheriff deputies just arrived. I'm sure they'll track them down."

Peter sat down and took another sip of tea, "I was only around the Eagans for a little while, but my heart really goes out to them. They're going through a lot."

Alfred nodded, but said nothing.

"I'm going to check on them tomorrow. With Elizabeth and the twins out of town, I have some rare flexibility. I want to be sure Daniel is okay and."

Peter's words trailed into thought as he watched the dark orange slice of the setting sun behind the silhouette of the downtown buildings. What a long day it had been. He remembered his concerns that morning were tight deadlines for his summer research project and a rash on his son's back. Now, there was so much more to deal with. But he was at peace.

He sat in silent musings as the last rays of orange sunlight disappeared in the dark grey horizon of downtown Columbia.

The next morning

Peter was up fairly early for a Saturday morning. With his family out of town, he'd planned on a day of yard work. Not everyone enjoyed this kind of thing, but he loved mowing the grass and working on his little garden of tomatoes and peppers.

Then there was the "clutter project" he and Elizabeth had been working on for months. How could a room be filled with so much stuff? He thought to himself as he ran his hand across the top of his bald head, closing the door to the "junk" room he hoped would become his home office. But with the events of the day before, all these things had to be set aside for now.

He took the last sip of his coffee and closed his Bible. He had just read the end of Luke 10, verses Alfred had recommended the night before.

He rested his head on the back of his recliner and thought of Mary and Martha, the two sisters mentioned in the passage.

Martha was worried and bothered by all she had to do. Peter related with her, but he wanted to be like her sister, Mary. Mary sat at the feet of Jesus, listening to His words.

Peter spent some time in prayer laying each concern, each task at Jesus' feet. As he did this, in his mind's eye, he could see a rushing river sweeping his burdens out of sight. He asked God to direct his steps as he looked forward to the day.

A few moments later, on the phone with Tammy Eagan

"So, it's okay if I swing by?" Peter asked Tammy, as he gathered his wallet and keys. "It's not too early."

"Heavens no," Tammy replied. "The deputies have already been here questioning Daniel and I'm brewing the second pot of coffee."

"Great, I should be there in less than half an hour," Peter said, getting into his car and letting the roof down. "No news on Jacob, yet?"

"No, but I did have something strange happen a few minutes ago, when I tried calling him," Tammy replied. "Someone else answered his phone. Some guy said Jacob wasn't available, but he wouldn't tell me why."

"That's strange," Peter replied. "I wonder who it was."

"I guess we can sort it all out when you get here," Tammy replied.

As Peter traveled the interstate to the Eagans with his convertible top down, the summer morning breeze was cool and refreshing as it whipped past his face.

He couldn't get his mind off of what Tammy said about her phone call to Jacob. Did he deliver the letter to Sarah or not?

When he arrived at the Eagan's house, Cassie greeted him. "Can you go check on Jacob? I think something's happened to him."

"Cassie!" Tammy said, easing her aside so Peter could enter the foyer. "We can't ask Dr. Anderson to travel to Charleston. Sorry about that Peter. Cassie can't stop asking about Sarah and Jacob."

"Actually, I've been wondering a lot about that very thing," Peter admitted as he followed Tammy into the kitchen.

"How about a fresh cup of coffee?" she asked.

"That sounds great," Peter said. "Where's Daniel? I'd love to meet him."

"He and Daddy went to retrieve the other letter and map he hid from the guy who kidnapped him," Cassie answered.

TWELVE

Tammy fixed Peter a cup of coffee and brought it to him where he was sitting with Cassie on the family's back porch.

The summer morning was still cool and a male cardinal was celebrating the day. Peter could hear a sound of running water, like a brook outside the porch door.

"What's that sound?" Peter asked. "Is there a stream right outside?"

"That's Hank's pride and joy," Tammy exclaimed. "If he'd put half the tender care into his family that he put into his garden fountain, things would've turned out a lot different in the Eagan household."

As soon as Tammy said it, she regretted it. It was a standard comeback; almost a knee jerk reaction. Only recently had she realized how much pinned up bitterness she had toward Hank. What bad timing, she thought. Hank seems to have finally taken his role as a father seriously and she was realizing how mad she was at him.

"So, he made the brook," Peter replied, standing and walking over to the porch door and looking out. "Wow! That's impressive. I love that sound. I'll have to ask him how he built it when he gets back. There's some fish too."

As Peter stepped outside to get a closer look, the Eagan's phone rang and Tammy excused herself to answer it.

"Do you want to feed the fish?" Cassie asked.

"Sure. How many do you have? I see three."

"There should be one more," Cassie called back, as she disappeared around the corner.

She emerged a few moments later with a handful of fish food and handed some to Peter. As they sprinkled food and watched the excitement of the fish, the fourth koi, a white one, emerged from under a rock.

"That was the sheriff's office," Tammy said through the screened porch door. "They found out where the man who kidnapped Daniel lives. He lives with his mom on the other side of the woods, off Lincreek Road. His name is Bubba. His mom says he has a learning disability and dropped out of middle school. She hasn't seen him for the last couple of days, but thought she may have heard him come in and leave last night."

"How do they know it's him?" Peter asked, as he emptied the rest of the fish food into the main pool.

"They followed his tracks and talked with his mother. She confirmed he disappears in the woods for sometimes days at a time. They have an APB out on him."

"What's an APB?" Cassie asked.

"An all-points bulletin," Peter answered. "It means everybody is looking for him."

"I'm scared!" Cassie said, following Peter back into the porch.

Tammy wrapped her arms around Cassie and pulled her close.

"Can Daddy stay again tonight?"

"We'll see honey."

Back on the porch, Tammy was heating up Peter's cup of coffee, when they heard car doors slam in front.

"Daddy's back," Cassie yelled and disappeared into the house.

In a moment, everyone converged in the den.

"We saw them!" Daniel exclaimed. "We saw the grave sites Jacob wrote about in his letter."

Tammy and Peter looked over at Hank as if to get a confirmation and he nodded, unfolding the map.

"They're right here," Hank unfolded the map on the coffee table and pointed to a place on it right before Hope Creek emptied into the Broad River. "This area next to the dirt road is thick with switch cane and there are pines and cedars along the creek bank. Unless you know to walk through the cane and between the trees you'd never see 'em. We saw only about twenty-five of them, mostly among the thicket on the other side of the creek. We uncovered a couple over half buried in the creek bed where the water is low. I'm sure we could have found more, but we wanted to get back."

"So, you think that's why Daniel was kidnapped, because he was looking for the graves?" Peter asked.

"I don't know," Hank replied. "The whole thing is so strange. It was just like Jacob's letter said. All the graves were marked with the same year, 1749. And all had last names of Hope or the letter 'H'."

"May I see the letter from Jacob?" Peter asked.

Hank handed it to him.

"Where'd you hide the map, Danny?" Cassie asked.

"I was in the switch … What did you call them, Dad?"

"Switch cane; it looks like bamboo, but more like sugar cane."

"I was in the switch cane when I heard someone coming up," Daniel continued. "So, I hid the papers under a moss-covered rock."

Peter studied the letter Jacob wrote to Dr. Shuler and the short hand-written note:

June 17th, 1940

Keep the map hidden. It marks the beginning of the crusade to wipe out the invaders. Continue what was begun and wipe them out until no Hope remains.

Luke

"Jacob wrote in his letter that his uncle Luke wrote this note," Peter said. "He was afraid his family was involved."

"First of all, how could a feud against a family be so intense that so many were killed?" Tammy asked. "And second of all, why are people still angry over 200 years later?"

"That's the question," Peter said. "The Luke guy called the Hopes invaders."

"Like space invaders?" Cassie asked quickly.

"No, Cassie. We're not saying space invaders. Your imagination knows no bounds. I like that honey, but don't let it cause you to be afraid."

Peter realized he should stop discussing the letter in front of Cassie and walked back into the sun room. He looked out into the Eagan's wooded back yard and took a sip of coffee, staring out in thought. Then he walked back into the den.

"We still haven't heard anything from Jacob Younginer," Peter said. "I think I'm going to drive down to Kiawah and see if I can figure out what happened to him. His phone's going right to voice mail when I try to call. And I want to be sure Sarah is okay, no matter how she responds to Jacob's letter."

"Can I go too?" Cassie erupted.

"No," Tammy said firmly.

"But I want to know what Sarah said," Cassie insisted.

"I'll call you guys as soon as I find out something," Peter insisted.

Peter said his goodbyes and headed to his house to pick up a few things before leaving for Kiawah.

When Peter arrived at his house, he was surprised to see Jimmy and Stephen Davis rocking on his front porch, waiting for him.

In the meantime, back in Irmo, at the Eagan's house

"This doesn't sound like a very good idea to me Hank," Tammy said forcefully. "We just got our son back and now you want to put him back into harm's way."

"Tammy, if you feel so strongly about it, I'll deliver the letter to Dr. Shuler myself," Hank said, beginning to feel that tense, 'no win' feeling in his stomach. "I promised Peter Anderson I would deliver the letter for Jacob and I just thought Daniel might enjoy going too."

"Mom, I'd really like to go," Daniel said. "We're just dropping off a letter."

"What if the deputies need to see the letter to help track down the man who took Daniel?"

"Then we'll tell them Dr. Shuler has it," Hank said, trying to remain calm.

Tammy finally conceded. She was partially afraid of getting further mixed up in the whole mess, but she was also thankful Hank was taking the initiative to do something with Daniel.

A short time later Hank and Daniel set out to deliver the letter.

"That says Selwood," Daniel pointed out as Hank slowed down and turned into the drive way off Old Bush River. "It's weird that it just says Selwood with no street or number."

"That is strange."

The house was wooden, painted white, with a Southern style green roof and matching shutters. It had a magnificent wrap around front porch, supported by finely crafted columns. There were matching white rocking chairs where Hank imagined many an afternoon was spent enjoying the beauties of the wooded lot. He thought the house had to have been built early in the last century if not before.

"Maybe it's because it was built a long time ago and there weren't many houses around then and that's all the address that was needed," Hank surmised.

He and Daniel got out of the car and climbed the stained dark wood porch steps. As they stepped, Daniel noticed the glossy shine yielded a reflection of his shoes.

The front porch reminded Hank of his childhood when he used to "watch the world go by" on the front porch of his grandparent's house.

Hank reached out to ring the doorbell, but before he could, the front door opened and a stately looking man in his late fifties, with salt and pepper hair and a nicely trimmed beard, appeared.

"I hope you aren't selling anything," the gentleman exclaimed. "It's way too early for that, and I'm so not interested. It's still coffee time on a Saturday morning."

"No sir," Hank replied. "We're sorry to disturb you, but we actually have a delivery for a Dr. Shuler at this address. My son here found a letter in an old shack in the woods behind our house. It was never opened, and we are assuming never delivered. My name is Hank Eagan and this is my son, Daniel."

"Are you Dr. Shuler?" Daniel asked.

"Yes I am, son."

Daniel held out the envelope with the map, the letter from Jacob and the note from his uncle, stuffed inside.

"A letter huh," Dr. Shuler said, taking it from Daniel. "Never opened?"

"Yes, Dr. Shuler," Hank admitted. "My son wants to talk to you about that."

Dr. Shuler looked at Daniel and could see his anguish. He tried to remain stern, but couldn't help a slight smile. He stood aside and motioned for him to step inside to the foyer. "Come on inside."

Dr. Shuler led them through a majestic formal living room with ten foot ceilings.

"Mary, we have some guests." Dr. Shuler called down the hall. "Please pour some coffee and juice."

"Have you had breakfast?"

"Not exactly, Dr. Shuler. But please don't go to any trouble for us," Hank said, looking around at the grandeur of the old house.

"I assure you, cooking is never a trouble for my Mary. She stands ready to offer culinary pleasures. You might say it's her gift."

"Honey, do you mind making us a batch of cinnamon toast?" he called to her, as they entered the side porch.

Hank was stunned at the Shuler's gorgeous yard. It was like a picture from a magazine: deep green grass garden bordered by monkey grass and river rocks surrounded by an explosion of midsummer floral colors of bright reds, blues and yellows.

"Make yourselves comfortable. I'll be back in a few minutes."

Dr. Shuler left the porch and returned moments later with two steaming mugs of coffee and a glass of orange juice he gave to Daniel.

"I wasn't sure what you took in your coffee," Dr. Shuler mentioned as he placed the tray on the coffee table next to where Hank was seated. "Here's cream, sugar and some sugar substitute."

Dr. Shuler sat down, grabbed his cup and turned squarely toward Daniel. "Did you want to say something to me son?"

Daniel shot an angry glance at his dad for putting him in the situation and then looked down.

There was an awkward pause, but neither Hank nor Dr. Shuler seemed willing to fill it.

"I shouldn't have," Daniel began, looking up at Dr. Shuler and then back down. "I shouldn't have opened your letter."

There was another pause.

"I'm sorry I did it," Daniel finally said. He looked up at Dr. Shuler and their eyes briefly met.

"Son," Dr. Shuler said. "If I was in your position, I'm pretty sure I would have done the same thing. But for what it's worth, I forgive you."

Dr. Shuler walked over to Daniel and asked him to stand up. When he did, their eyes met again and Dr. Shuler extended his hand for a handshake.

"When you can admit you're wrong, no matter how difficult, you begin to take steps toward manhood," Dr Shuler said.

Daniel returned the handshake and then Dr. Shuler said, "My wife's feeling a little under the weather. I'll be back in a moment with the toast."

While the doctor was in the kitchen helping his wife, Hank loaded up his coffee with sugar and cream. He really appreciated what Dr. Shuler had said to Daniel. He wished he had words of wisdom like that to give his son.

Before Dr. Shuler returned, the aroma of the sweet cinnamon wafted into the porch where the Eagan boys were enjoying their beverages. Daniel could feel his mouth begin to water.

"You two are in for a treat! Take a bite of one of these," Dr. Shuler stated as he set the platter down in front of his guests."

Hank reached down and picked up one of the dark brown squares of wheat toast and took a bite. As he did, the savory mixture of crystallized cinnamon sugar and rich creamy butter flowed around his tongue and flooded his taste buds with delight.

"Wow!" Hank looked up at Dr. Shuler and then over at Daniel, who was also completing his first bite, eyes wide with enjoyment.

Dr. Shuler grinned in satisfaction at the enjoyment his wife's cooking had yielded. "I told you, you were in for a treat. Mary calls it carmelization. I don't think it's really a word, but it happens when she toasts the bread a bit first, then adds melted butter before sprinkling on cinnamon, freshly scraped off the stick, mixed with sugar."

When they completed their first piece, Dr Shuler offered them another. Then turning to Daniel,

he said, "So you found this letter in an old shack?"

Daniel went on to explain how he and Cassie had found some letters a couple of days before. Daniel also told the story of being kidnapped, and in doing so, he mentioned for the first time that he heard his kidnapper speaking to someone on the phone named MB.

As Hank watched Daniel tell of his kidnapping, he sensed that reliving it was hard for him.

"Where does the name Selwood originate, Dr. Shuler?" Hank asked after Daniel was through telling his story, trying to lighten the mood.

"You can call me Bill," he replied. "My family migrated here from Pennsylvania between the Broad and Saluda Rivers in the mid 1700s. This was before the Lake Murray dam, of course, and the area was a valley. 'Selwood' comes from the Swiss word Zell, which means valley."

"I like to learn more about the history of an area," Hank replied. "It's fascinating to know about days gone by."

"Yes, I love history as well." Dr. Shuler took another sip of coffee and slid the documents out of the envelope and began shuffling through and reading the pages.

Dr. Shuler unfolded the last note from Jacob's uncle Luke, read it and placed it carefully on the table with the other documents.

"Do you know Jacob Younginer?" Hank asked.

THIRTEEN

Dr. Shuler looked straight ahead, his gray mustache hiding his tightly drawn lips.

"I know the family name," he replied.

Hank couldn't help but feel as if Dr. Shuler wanted to say more, but didn't.

"My mother's maiden name was Hope before she married my dad, Stephen Shuler," Dr. Shuler said. "Her brother's name was George, Dr. George Hope. George was much younger than my mother and…"

Dr. Shuler looked at Hank and then glanced at Daniel.

"I'm not sure I should be talking about all this," Dr. Shuler said; "especially in front of the boy."

Hank looked over at Daniel and then replied. "It's okay. He's pretty mature for his age. He can handle it."

Hank picked up on a quick twinkle in Daniel's eye and a slight grin.

"George and his wife Annie were married at Pilgrim Lutheran, across the dam from here," Dr. Shuler pointed. "Uncle George had just completed his residency and after their honeymoon he and Aunt Annie were to leave for Chad in central Africa as missionaries. Aunt Annie was going to set up a school to help educate the children and Uncle George was to set up medical dispensaries near various villages and train the locals in basic nursing skills."

Dr. Shuler paused and took another sip of coffee.

"Uncle George was found dead, upstairs in this very house, two days after they returned from their honeymoon. This is the home I grew up in and Mom and Dad were letting them stay here as they prepared to leave for Africa. I had already left for college, so I don't know all the details, but the death was ruled a heart attack.

My mother has not spoken much about any of this during all these years since Uncle George's death but has always thought he was drugged. She told me once that Uncle George had been out to eat supper with an old high school classmate the night before he died. Aunt Annie had already gone to bed when Uncle George came home from his dinner, but mom was up reading. She said Uncle George acted like he was drunk or something, but he was not a drinking man.

She pressed the issue with the police, but they wouldn't even consider foul play as a possibility. To this day, she thinks the whole thing was a planned murder and cover up."

"To this day?" Hank replied. "So your mom's still alive?"

"Yes, she lives in a nursing home a few miles from here," Dr. Shuler replied, pointing towards downtown Irmo. "Her health's not good. She won't talk much about what happened to Uncle George or Aunt Annie. Probably a good thing.

I've never seen anyone so distraught! Uncle George was her little brother and since she was so much older, she mothered him."

"You said your mother won't talk about your uncle or your aunt. Did something happen to your Aunt Annie as well?" Daniel asked.

Dr. Shuler paused a moment as if wondering if he should be giving these details, but then continued, "After Uncle George died, Aunt Annie discovered she was pregnant. She moved in with her parents in Clinton. Mom would often visit her.

When it came time for her to give birth, there were complications. The baby was breach and they had to do an emergency caesarian. Aunt Annie had a problem with her blood clotting and she bled to death.

The baby, a little boy, lived. Mom and Aunt Annie's parents found a couple to adopt him."

"How's he doing now?" Hank asked.

"Mom won't talk about him. I don't even know where he ended up. I have a younger cousin I've never met and Mom won't even tell me his name."

"What does she say when you ask her?" Daniel asked.

"Nothing," Dr. Shuler said looking out into the garden. "She says nothing."

Meanwhile, at Peter's house in Forest Acres

"Here we go again," Peter said to himself, as he saw Jimmy and Stephen sitting on his front porch as he turned into the driveway from his visit with the Eagans. "I wonder what they want."

"I thought you were mad it me?" Peter said to Jimmy, as he approached the porch.

"I was mad, Doc," Jimmy admitted. "I couldn't understand why you would black ball me from the meteorite experiment when you knew it was what I wanted the most. I felt betrayed. The wounds of a friend are far worse than those of an enemy."

Peter sat down on a bench across from the rocking chairs.

"So how are you now?" Peter asked.

"I'm better," Jimmy replied. "I had a great conversation with Stephen and Marlee last night. But before I tell you about it, you don't happen to have some of that fresh orange juice Elizabeth squeezes? I've been bragging to Stephen about how good it is and he doesn't believe me."

Peter smiled. "Unfortunately for you, and Stephen, Elizabeth is out of town. So, we can't have refills, but she did squeeze enough for me for the weekend and I'm willing to share."

Peter returned after a few minutes with three small breakfast glasses full of freshly squeezed orange juice and handed them out.

"Wow!" Stephen commented after a large sip. "That is so good!"

"I get a glass every morning," Peter admitted. "Elizabeth says she's spoiling me. And I guess she's right. We've been through a lot of ups and downs in our marriage. But we've maintained certain ceremonial expressions of love as often as we can."

"I'll have to talk to my wife about doing this," Stephen said. "I even like the fact that the pulp is still in it."

"Yea, sometimes people strain the pulp out, but I like it. Plus, Elizabeth tells me it adds fiber. Oh, and on asking your wife to squeeze you orange juice," Peter continued. "You might want to start by doing something for her. These expressions of love I'm talking about can't be contrived. They must be spontaneous. Fix her tea or coffee in the morning. That's a good start."

Stephen nodded and took another sip.

"Okay, Jimmy, back to you. Tell me about your conversation with Marlee and Stephen last night.

"Well, they helped me understand that all of you played a part in blocking me from the meteorite research and they helped me understand why. I was a little angry at all of you for a while, but finally understood the necessity."

"A little angry?" Stephen piped in. "That might be an understatement."

"You're right," Jimmy admitted. "I was very angry, but we talked it through.

I know now the full result of what would have been a reality if you all hadn't done what you did."

"I'm glad you understand, Jimmy," said Peter. "And I do accept your apology. Is that why you're here?"

"One of the reasons," Stephen replied.

"I kind of expected that," Peter grinned. "Go on."

"Well, with some recent developments over the last 24 hours, we're very close to being able to repeat what you and Jimmy did a few years ago. Jimmy and I know that you disagree with anyone trying to 'fix' an event of life by sending a warning message back in time. However, as we discussed earlier, we have different views."

"Do you mean what you said on the phone about using the technology for good and how you compared it to saving a life with a heart transplant? And what you said about the responsibility to use technology for good, if it is in your power to wield it. Did I miss anything?"

"No, you summarized it well," said Stephen.

"So, since you have the abilities, you haven't come to ask for my help. Are you somehow asking for my permission?"

"No, not really, Doc," answered Jimmy. "We do recognize that what we will be attempting has much more risk than a heart transplant. We know from what happened before that we could potentially affect many more lives."

"And?" asked Peter.

"And," Stephen said. "We accept the greater risk as a reason to be ultra-careful in analyzing the event that we choose to reverse and the way we communicate it."

"Doc," said Jimmy. "We know you disagree with what we're doing, but before we do it, we wanted to let you know so that you wouldn't think we were going behind your back."

Peter looked at Jimmy but said nothing.

"We wanted you to know we hear your concerns," Stephen said.

Realizing that Jimmy and Stephen's minds were made up, Peter decided to drop the subject. He invited them in for some of Elizabeth's muffins.

"What does the rest of your day look like," Jimmy asked, as Peter handed him a banana nut muffin. "You have a rare weekend off. Would you like to come have supper with Marlee and me?"

"I appreciate that Jimmy, but I'm heading to Kiawah to check on Sarah. I was introduced to an old boyfriend of hers yesterday. He went to check on her and I haven't heard back from him."

"I'm actually heading to Kiawah myself," Stephen said, taking a bite of muffin. "I need to grab some things from home. It looks like I'll be in Columbia for a while."

"I thought you said you lived in Charleston," Peter said.

"I usually say Charleston because people have heard of it, but I actually own a small condo on Kiawah Island. Here's my card. Call me if you get a chance. I'm heading there after I drop Jimmy off."

Peter took Stephen's card and walked with his colleagues to the front porch.

"All I can say to you two is hold on to your seats," Peter warned as they were getting into Stephen's car. "You have chosen to take on a tornado by changing an event that's already occurred and you have no idea which way the winds will blow."

FOURTEEN

As Peter watched Jimmy and Stephen drive off, he couldn't help but pray, "Lord, please protect us all from what Jimmy and Stephen plan to do. I ask you to please thwart their plans. Please keep them from being able to send a message back in time and to change an event. You're teaching me to bring every concern before your throne. You are my King. You are the Master, weaving the events of life together, one thread connected to many others. I know you are sovereign, even when man's technology leads into uncharted waters. Amen"

Having done all he could and having given the burden to God, he determined to take Alfred's advice and not fret about it anymore.

He decided that when Jimmy and Stephen's experiment came to mind, he would simply pray for peace and for God's will to be done.

He completed a couple of chores, gathered up some lunch to eat on the way, called Elizabeth and hit the highway to Kiawah Island.

Meanwhile, in Irmo at the Eagan's

"Hey Mom, Daniel and Daddy are back," Cassie called out as she heard the car door close.

Tammy slowly rose from her bed and glanced in the mirror over the chest of drawers in the bedroom she used to share with Hank. She wiped a tear. She knew what she was about to say and do was going to crush Cassie. But she had to follow her heart. What she didn't know was how much it would affect Hank and even Daniel.

As much as she had recognized a change in Hank, she couldn't get over the years his obsession with work had cost their family. He had walked out on them and she had no way of knowing if he would do it again. She had to protect Cassie's heart and her own. The more Hank was around, the harder it would be when and if he left again.

When she got downstairs Hank and Daniel were talking about the beauty of the old Selwood house, the garden and the cinnamon toast.

"It was buttery and crispy," Daniel declared.

"Did you bring me some?" Cassie asked.

"Actually, we did," Hank grinned and nodded to Daniel.

Daniel revealed a bag he had been hiding behind his back and took out some wax paper in which Mrs. Shuler had carefully wrapped a piece of toast. He handed it to Cassie.

"There's one in here for you too, Mom."

Daniel smiled as he handed the bag to his mom.

Tammy couldn't remember the last time there were smiles when the four of them were together. Was she doing the right thing?

Daniel and Hank proceeded to tell the girls what they had learned about Dr. Shuler's uncle's death and the subsequent birth of his child.

"The mom died too," Daniel replied sadly. "But the baby boy lived."

"Where is he?" Cassie asked.

"Dr. Shuler doesn't know," Hank answered. "He was put up for adoption, but his mom won't tell him where he ended up."

"So, he's a Hope?" Tammy asked.

"Technically he is," Hank said. "But I'm sure he took on another name."

"I'd like to talk to Dr. Shuler's mom," Daniel said. "He says she lives in a nursing home in Irmo."

"This is all very interesting," Tammy said, seizing a brief pause in the conversation, but I need to talk to your dad. "Hank, please step outside with me a second."

"Uh Oh," Hank grinned. "I feel like I'm in trouble."

"I bet they're getting back together," Cassie said, looking in the direction of the front door they just walked out of.

"I wouldn't be so sure," Daniel warned, half protectively and half as an opportunity to dig his sister. "Mom hasn't looked too happy lately."

"They seem to be getting along better, though," Cassie offered. "It's been great having Dad here without a whole bunch of yelling."

In a few moments Hank and Tammy entered the foyer from outside and Hank went quickly towards the downstairs bedroom he had stayed in the night before.

"Where's Dad going?" Cassie asked.

"He's leaving, Sweetie." Tammy said, pulling her close.

"Why? I don't want him to. Daddy!" Cassie struggled to pull away and go after him, but Tammy held her.

"Mom, let me go. Why is Dad leaving?"

"Because I asked him to, Sweetheart. I don't want him to break our hearts again."

"No Mom! If you don't want to break my heart, then don't ask him to leave."

Cassie pulled away and went crying upstairs.

Tammy chased after her.

Daniel stood watching from the entrance to the kitchen.

Meanwhile, at Charleston Memorial Hospital

"He's got a bad concussion," the doctor said to the nurse who was checking Jacob's blood sugar.

"Hovering near 500," the nurse said. "He must be a diabetic, but he's not wearing a necklace or bracelet."

"I bet your right," the doctor agreed. "The glucose in the transfusion is driving his numbers up."

"A deputy is waiting to talk to him if we can get him alert enough," A second nurse said as she entered.

The doctor acknowledged her with a nod and the asked the other nurse?

"You say he was screaming something a little while ago?"

"Yes, about twenty minutes ago he started screaming, 'Sarah, Sarah'. He even opened his eyes for a brief moment. He was very agitated."

"Give him 15 units of Novalog," the doctor said. "I don't know if he's on insulin or not, but we need to get his glucose levels down. Check him again in about 30 minutes and let me know."

"I will," the nurse said as she gave Jacob the units of insulin the doctor ordered.

Meanwhile, at the Security Gate into Kiawah Island

After a pleasant drive to the coast, Peter pulled out the business card Stephen had given him and gave him a call.

When Stephen answered he said, "Stephen, this is Peter. Are you on the island yet?"

"Just got here. How about you?"

"I'm at the security gate. I forgot all about it. Can you get me in?"

"Sure thing. In fact, I just mentioned to my wife that you would be down here and we insist that you stay with us."

"I'm not even sure I'll be staying the night, but that's mighty nice of you. Where's your condo?"

"We are at 125 Baffin Bay, right before the turn to The Sanctuary."

"That's not far from where Sarah's condo is. I might stop by if that's okay. I've had several cups of coffee and it's been a long ride. If you know what I mean."

"You are welcome to use our facilities," Stephen laughed. "I'll call the security gate and leave you a pass."

"That's great," Peter said. "See you in a minute."

FIFTEEN

"Dr. Anderson!" Stephen said a few minutes later as he opened the door and motioned Peter in. Who would have thought we would meet again so soon. Step right this way. You mentioned your first order of business was to visit the facilities."

Stephen ushered Peter into a hallway off the foyer and into the downstairs restroom.

After a few minutes, Peter emerged with a countenance of immense relief.

"You look better already," Stephen said handing Peter a tall glass of sweet tea with lemon.

"Already priming me to make a return visit, huh Davis?" Peter smiled accepting the glass. "To let you know, once you pass middle age, you become much more familiar with rooms of relief such as that one."

"I'm beginning to experience the same pattern."

Both men laughed as Stephen led them into the living room. "Sit for a moment and finish your tea. Sounds like you are on an adventure of your own."

"Been sitting for a while," Peter said walking toward the sliding glass doors in the back of the room. He noticed a wooded path leading down to the beach.

"But I will sit a minute and finish this tea."

"Stay as long as you'd like. I have no plans today other than seeing what comes my way."

Peter nodded and then said, "This is great tea, you didn't brew it did you Davis?"

"You know me well. No, Jean brewed it this morning. She's off playing tennis, but sends her regards."

"Give her my best and tell her how much I'm enjoying her tea."

"I'll tell her," Stephen said, sitting down in an overstuffed brown leather chair with his own glass of tea.

"This place amazes me," Peter mused, looking out at the afternoon sun through the trees. "What a hidden paradise; forest paths and shady trees leading right up to the edge of white sand beaches and a brilliant blue ocean. No wonder they set a guard up to keep the rest of us out."

"You can be our guest any time," Stephen replied. "We have two bedrooms. You and Elizabeth name the weekend. We'd love to have you."

"No talk about the time experiments if we come, right?" Peter added, only half joking.

"I promise," Stephen answered. "Don't worry, Anderson, we learned from you. You're the pioneer. We just want to make it better. Think back at the massive amounts of innovation over the last hundred and fifty years. Back then electricity, telegraphy and gas lighting was in its infancy. We have come so far and made it over so many hurdles. There were almost always hic-ups and periods of improvements with new technology. I'm sure Tesla and Edison had some reservations about the use of electricity when their experiments resulted in the 5th Avenue laboratory fire of 1895. But I'm glad they didn't stop there."

Peter looked at Stephen, half aggravated that he took this opportunity to continue his justification of their experiments, but half seeing the validity in what he was saying. He smiled and said, "So I take it your promise you just made to not talk about your experiments starts now."

Stephen, realizing the irony of Peter's remarks, smiled as well.

"Tell me more about your visit and what's going on with Sarah," Stephen said, changing the subject.

Peter told him about the suspicious guy named Matt Sarah had hooked up with, the letter from Jacob Younginer and Jacob's quest to find Sarah and deliver the undelivered letter to her personally.

"And we haven't heard from Jacob since he came down here to find Sarah yesterday," Peter said finishing up his glass of tea and setting it on the bar that separated the den area from the kitchen. "And what makes matters worse is that somebody has Jacob's phone."

"So, you say Sarah's place is at Mariner's Watch?" Stephen said, not expecting an answer. "That's only a few blocks down. If you want, you can leave your car here and walk down. In fact, do you mind if I go with you? If there's trouble, I'd hate for you to be alone."

"Sure, that would be great," Peter answered.

"Okay, let me write Jean a note and throw on some shoes. I'll be right back."

Peter walked over to the doors that led to the deck and walked out into the warm sun. The shade and ocean wind made it pleasant in spite of the season. He still wasn't sure he entirely trusted Stephen, but he was happy for the company.

"How long have you lived here?" Peter asked as they passed rows of condos and walked along a dark wood chip mulched path past Palmetto trees to a wooden sign that read neatly in white embossed letters, 'Mariner's Watch'.

"We invested in the condo two years ago," Stephen answered. "And we couldn't be happier with it."

"I can see why," Peter said, fighting a feeling of envy.

"Did you say the Condo belongs to Sarah?" Stephen asked, as they followed the wooded path to the left onto Mariner's Watch Road.

"It actually belongs to her mom, but I haven't seen her since Benjamin's funeral."

After a few more minutes, Peter and Stephen knocked on the condo door and heard footsteps.

Meanwhile, back in Columbia at his apartment near Finlay Park

"Back to watery tuna fish sandwiches," Hank said out loud as he ate at his favorite lonely perch overlooking the fountain in front of his apartment building.

"I know you're happy about that," he called down to the eager cat already lopping up the tuna drippings and hoping for more. "But I'm not happy. I was ready to go home. I guess I waited too long. Tammy has turned sour toward me."

Hank felt horrible. He was glad Daniel was safe and that he had had some really meaningful conversations with him for the first time in what seemed like years. It felt odd that it took Daniel's kidnapping to make him feel a part of his own family again.

He ate a few more bites then dropped the mess to the cement below. The cat, hearing the plop, rushed over to enjoy it.

"Still haven't tried to drain the water?" Alfred said, moving from behind Hank and sitting down beside him.

"There you are again, neighbor, sneaking up on me," Hank said forcing a smile. "Yeah, I forgot about your advice to drain the tuna water. But I didn't forget about the other advice you gave me?"

"Which was?"

"You suggested that I try and listen to Daniel's heart and not take everything so personally."

"How did it go? You don't look like things have gone very well since I last saw you."

"The part with Daniel was the highlight, but things didn't end well, at least for Tammy and me."

Hank thought about ending the story there, but looking over at Alfred and seeing what appeared to be concern, he continued.

"Daniel was actually missing for a while, kidnapped. He's safe now, but I was really worried about him. I think it helped me understand how much I really care about him. I'm ashamed at how I let my crap and insecurities get in the way of loving my family."

"It's amazing how tragedies can put things into perspective," Alfred commented.

"And I think, he saw it too," Hank continued. "I think he saw that I care. We went out together this morning to visit a neighbor and it felt like a father/son adventure. We had a blast."

I spent the night at the house last night and we were all together, just like it's supposed to be. It felt like my home again. Cassie was so happy! And maybe even Daniel. I was going to stay again tonight, but it wasn't to be."

"What happened?"

"Pretty soon after Daniel and I got back from visiting Dr. Shuler, our neighbor, Tammy called me out of the room to talk. I could tell she'd been crying."

Hank looked down, remembering the conversation, then continued.

"Seems while I was warming up to the idea of coming back home, Tammy was growing cold to it. She's afraid for Cassie, particularly. My leaving tore her up and Tammy doesn't want to get her hopes up and then have me leave again or do something stupid and hurt everybody."

"What do you think?" Alfred asked. "Do you think you would break her heart again?"

"I certainly don't want to. But I didn't want to hurt her the first time."

Hank looked ahead at the fountain and the afternoon sun starting its downward approach to the skyline of the capital city. Tears welled up in his eyes, thinking of how he caused his little girl such pain.

"I'm happy to have had that brief connection with Daniel, but in a way it's making the whole thing worse."

"How so?"

"This morning, going out together, just the two of us, was something I've longed for with him," Hank looked up at Alfred. "And it happened so naturally. It flowed out of the caring I realized I have for him. Too bad I didn't realize it until today."

"What are you going to do?" Alfred asked after a few minutes of silence.

"I'm going to fight."

"Fight what?"

"Fight for my family. I'm going to do everything I can to have thousands of more days like to today; with Cassie, with Daniel and especially with Tammy. I just hate I made such a mess of things before I realized how rich a man I am, or was."

"It's not too late to show them you love them," Alfred said. "Who knows if Tammy will take you back? But if you fight for your family's hearts, just like you are saying, regardless of how you are treated, they will begin to realize you really do love them."

Hank nodded. "It's going to be a challenge showing them my love when I'm not living there. But I think I'm ready for another adventure."

Alfred smiled and put his hand on Hank's shoulder. "Hank, do you mind if I pray for you and your family."

Hank shook his head. "No, I don't mind." But as he said it, he was stunned the words were coming out of his mouth.

Alfred prayed for Hank to remain steadfast in his love for his family and he prayed that Tammy, Daniel and Cassie would receive his love and begin to trust it. It was a short prayer, but Hank really appreciated it.

Soon after the prayer was over, Hank's phone rang. He didn't recognize the number, but excused himself from Alfred and answered the call as he stepped away, "Hello."

"Hank? This is Bill, Bill Shuler."

"Yes, Dr. Shuler. How are you?"

"I'm fine. Thanks. I hope you are. Listen, I went by to visit my mother this morning. And I told her about your visit."

"Oh yeah. Good. Did she have a response?"

"She didn't say much. But she did write a letter while I was there. And she wants to get it to Jacob Younginer. Would you be willing to give it to him when you find him?"

"Yes. Dr. Shuler. I'll be glad to do that. Do you have the letter?"

"Yes, I do."

"Okay, I'll stop by and get it soon."

SIXTEEN

Peter and Stephen stood in anticipation as footsteps stopped just on the other side of the closed condo door.

"Who is it?" a frail voice asked through the wood.

"It's Peter, Peter Anderson."

"Peter!"

The door immediately swung open and Mrs. Jenkins, Sarah's mom, stood in the doorway.

"Peter, I can't believe you're here. Come on in."

"Hello Mrs. Jenkins," Peter responded, as he stepped into the foyer followed by Stephen. "It's so nice to see you. I haven't seen you in years. This is a colleague of mine, Stephen Davis."

"Nice to meet you ma'am," Stephen extended his hand and Mrs. Jenkins took it and squeezed it.

"Peter, I'm really glad you're here," Mrs. Jenkins said leading them into small, but nicely furnished den. "Sarah's in trouble and I'm not sure how to help her."

"What do you mean?" Peter asked, glancing over at Stephen.

"For the last few months she's gotten mixed up with a man who is really bad news. She's not herself around him and he's always with her.

"She says she loves him. But I don't believe her."

"Why?"

"It's the way he treats her; very verbally abusive. I met him once when they showed up in Greenville together. They announced they were getting married and that they wanted to move down here to our condo."

"Are they married?"

"Not yet. And I told them I would not allow them shacking up down here. Sarah seemed like she understood and would respect my wishes. But before I know it, I find out from our neighbors here that she's been here with that man named Matt."

"Have you talked to her about it?"

"I've tried, but I can never talk to her alone, even on the phone. Matt is always with her. Something's wrong, Peter. He seems to have some power over her and she's miserable. I can see it in her eyes."

"Where are they now?" Peter asked.

"I don't know," Mrs. Jenkins responded. I arrived early yesterday evening to talk to them about disobeying my wishes and nobody was here. All Sarah's stuff is here, even her medication box. She never goes anywhere without it. Wherever she is, she left in a hurry. And she doesn't do well without her medication."

"Mr. Jenkins, have you heard Sarah talk about Jacob Younginer?"

"Jacob! Yes, of course. Sarah and Jacob were perfect together, at least until they broke up. He absolutely shattered her heart. I cared for Jacob, but I hated what he did to my daughter."

"Interesting you should say that," Peter said. "I met Jacob yesterday and it seems there has been some miscommunication between Jacob and Sarah. I think Sarah's conclusion about how Jacob feels about her is based on false information, or better said, lack of information. And Jacob came down here yesterday to find Sarah and try to straighten things out between them. At least he was headed this way."

"What happened?"

"Don't know. We've lost communication with him. We were hoping to find news of him here. I'm thinking of just calling some of the local hospitals to see if he's been admitted."

"Probably not a bad idea, Mrs. Jenkins," Peter said. "Matt Baston is bad news. I'm not waiting any longer. I'm calling the police."

Back at Finlay Park

"Is everything okay?" Alfred asked, as Hank returned to the bench after talking with Dr. Shuler.

"Yeah, seems I need to head back to Irmo. The neighbor Daniel and I talked to, Dr. Shuler, needs me to do something for him. He has a letter he's asked me to deliver.

"Are you going now?" Alfred asked.

"Might as well. I don't have anything else to do." Hank answered.

"Want some company?"

"Well, maybe so," Hank answered a bit hesitantly at first, but then added, "Yeah, that would be good. I could use some company."

"I might even upset the apple cart a bit and drive by the house," Hank said a few minutes later as he backed his car out of his slot in the parking garage. "Technically, this is my weekend to have the kids."

Alfred looked his way, but said nothing.

After Hank had navigated onto I-26 toward Irmo, he broke the silence. "You said your wife died recently, if you don't mind me asking how you've handled that; I'm sure that wasn't in the plans."

"It's been really hard. We worked at being together as much as we could. I really feel a part of me is missing.

"We did little things together all the time. We didn't even have to talk. We didn't have to do anything extraordinary. We just enjoyed being together, whatever we were doing."

"Even going shopping?"

Alfred looked over at Hank and smiled as they passed an old white station wagon nearing their exit. "Yes, even shopping. It wasn't my favorite activity, but we tried to make it fun. I tried to make a game of it. We'd split the list up and see who could finish first. We laughed a lot; mostly her laughing at my attempts to find the right aisles and get the best deals."

Alfred continued to smile as he thought of it.

"I hate shopping. I don't think I could handle that," Hank said as he veered onto the exit.

"You should try it." Alfred said.

"I don't think Tammy would even want me to go with her. She made that pretty clear this morning. I think this whole year I've been gone Tammy would have had me back when I was ready, but now that I think I am, she doesn't want me."

"Have you told her?"

"Told her what?"

"That you want to come back?"

"Not exactly; but I think she knows," Hank said, as he slowed to turn into Dr. Shuler's driveway.

Alfred didn't respond. He only nodded.

"I'll be right back," Hank said to Alfred as he parked in front of Dr. Shuler's house.

Hank admired the pink, purple, red and white impatience hanging symmetrically on hooks around the porch. He was thinking about what Alfred had asked as he walked up the shiny steps he and Daniel had ascended only a few hours before.

Dr. Shuler must've seen him drive up because the door was opened before Hank reached the top step.

"You made it here quickly," Dr. Shuler said.

"Yea, I had some time on my hands," Hank said, forcing a smile.

"Where's your buddy?"

The question had no place to land in Hank's mind at first, but then he caught it. Dr. Shuler was referring to Daniel. He'd always wanted Daniel to be his buddy, but it hadn't worked out that way, at least not yet.

"He's with his mom," Hank replied.

"I'm surprised he's not with you, you two seemed inseparable."

Really? Hank thought, but said nothing.

"Here you are," Dr. Shuler said, handing Hank a sealed letter. "Mom says that no one is to open this but Jacob Younginer. Her mind has been in and out lately, but I had a great discussion with her today. I was so glad to find her so lucid. I have no idea what the letter says and she wasn't willing to discuss it with me."

"I'll get it to him," Hank said, taking the letter and shaking it slightly with conviction.

"Do you know where he is?"

"Not yet, but I hope to know soon."

"If you don't find him, Mother wants you to bring the letter back unopened. She was pretty emphatic about it."

"Will do," Hank replied, sliding the letter in his back pocket and shaking Dr. Shuler's hand.

"Here's my number," Dr. Shuler said, handing him a card. "Call me as soon as you find him and deliver the letter. Mom wants to know he got it."

"Okay. I will."

Back in the car Hank pulled out a slip of paper with Peter Anderson's number on it.

"Excuse me just a moment," Hank said to Alfred. "I need to call somebody."

"Take your time," Alfred said. "I'm just along for the ride. I have nothing to do but hang out with you."

Hank cocked his head and looked at Alfred, thinking that to be a rather weird comment. But all the same, he liked it.

"Hello," said Peter when he answered Hank's call.

"Peter, this is Hank, Hank Eagan. How are things going?"

"Hey Hank," Peter replied. "Things are a bit rough down here. Sarah's missing and we're getting the police involved. How's Daniel?"

"He's okay, but I'm not with him now," Hank said. "Listen, have you found Jacob Younginer yet?"

"Not yet, Peter replied. A friend and I are checking the local hospitals to see if he's been admitted."

"Okay. Call me when you know more. Dr. Shuler has given me a letter to deliver to Jacob. And I need to make sure to get it in his hands."

"Okay, I'll let you know what we find out," Peter hung up and turned into the emergency room parking area at Charleston Memorial.

"Wow, Peter," Stephen replied. "I don't think you have ever referred to me as a friend."

"I appreciate you being here," Peter replied. "I'm really worried about Sarah. And I want Jacob to tell her how he feels. A whole lot seems to be coming against them, but I'd much rather Sarah end up with Jacob than this Matt Baston guy."

SEVENTEEN

"Thanks for driving," Peter said, as they got out of Stephen's car and headed toward the Emergency Room entrance. "You are much more familiar with this area than me."

"No problem. I certainly don't know all the details of what's going on, but from what I'm picking up, this is quite an unusual situation unfolding here; an undelivered letter, hearts torn apart and a villain in the midst. I couldn't find anything more alluring if I was watching a movie back at the condo."

"You're right about that, Davis," Peter said.

"You may have problems with HIPAA," Stephen said under his breath, as they approached the front desk."

"I was just thinking that," Peter replied.

"May I help you?" asked the attendant at the front desk.

"Yes," Peter began. "A friend of mine is missing and we are checking local hospitals to see if he has been admitted."

"I see," said the attendant. "What is your friend's name?"

"Jacob Younginer."

"We don't have anyone by that name." But then she hesitated and said, "Have a seat in the waiting area for a minute please."

At that, the attendant disappeared through the doors to the right of the front desk.

Stephen and Peter sat down and as if on queue, both called their wives to update them on where they were.

Back in Irmo, in Dr. Shuler's driveway

When Hank hung up from talking with Peter, he looked at Alfred and asked, "Would you like to meet my family?"

"I'd love too," Alfred replied, fastening his seat belt as Hank navigated around the Shuler's circular drive way.

From the bedroom window, Tammy saw Hank's car come to a stop in the driveway a few minutes later. Part of her was angry Hank had returned so soon after she asked him to leave, but she also felt a strange satisfaction that Hank seemed to be pursuing his family. Finally!

"Back so soon," she chided, as she opened the door before he and Alfred reached the front steps.

"Yes, I wanted you guys to meet my new friend," Hank replied, as he pointed in Alfred's direction. "Alfred, this is my wife, Tammy."

As he said it Hank looked directly in her eyes with a telling look.

Tammy couldn't help but notice the intensity of his glance as he emphasized the word 'wife', but quickly looked away and focused on Alfred.

"Pleased to meet you, Mrs. Eagan," Alfred said, nodding his head slightly in respect.

"Please, call me Tammy," she replied, noticing immediately the kindness in the old black man's eyes. "How do you know Hank?"

"We're neighbors," Alfred replied. "At least for now."

"For now?" Hank asked. "I thought you just moved in. Are you leaving again?"

"No, I'm not leaving," Alfred smiled, glancing at Hank.

Hank cocked his head curiously. Then, understanding what he meant, he smiled.

Tammy chose to ignore the comment and invited the two men in.

"Daddy!" Cassie emerged, bounding down the stairs and leaping into her father's arms from the second step.

"Hey Sweetie," Hank said as he caught her and twirled her around.

"Are you going to stay with us tonight?"

"Not tonight," Hank was quick to reply. "But, I'd like to introduce you to my new friend."

He set her down, and turned her toward Alfred.

"Honey, this is Mr. Alfred."

"Hey Mr. Alfred," Cassie smiled and extended her hand to give him a shake.

"As long as your parents are okay with it," Alfred said, glancing at them both. "You can call me Alfred."

Hank and Tammy nodded their approval then Hank said. "Alfred and I were wondering if you and Daniel would like to go grab a frozen yogurt. And you too Tammy, if you'd like."

"Out of the question, Hank," Tammy responded, surprising herself at the intensity of her emotions and her words. "It took me an hour to calm Cassie down after you left this morning. Why don't you and Alfred stay a few minutes and let's let that be all for one day. Every time you leave, it leaves a fresh cut on Cassie's wounded heart. And besides, Daniel isn't even here; He went down the street to visit Robert."

"Momma, please!" Cassie pleaded.

"No, I'm going to be firm with this honey. I don't think it's a good idea."

"Well technically," Hank began, realizing as he spoke that what he was about to say, was probably not a good idea. "This is my weekend to have the kids."

"Your weekend," Tammy's voice began to rise and continued it's climb. "Hank do you realize how many times I have wanted you to be a father to these kids and how many times you've left them disappointed when it was your weekend to spend time with them? Daniel's heart was crushed just as much as Cassie's every time you came up with some lame excuse why you couldn't pick them up."

Hank started to speak, but Tammy continued. "What awful excuses you came up with. Do you think we're stupid? At least it would have been honest if you'd just told us you didn't want to be around us?"

Hank couldn't help but realize Tammy was saying 'us', though she was speaking of the kids.

He started to speak again, but Tammy continued, even with Alfred standing there, she held nothing back. "Your weekend! So, when it's convenient and when you finally decide to be a husband and a father, you think you can just come in like everything is okay."

Embarrassed at allowing her pent up hurt out in front of Alfred, Tammy burst into tears and rushed upstairs.

"Momma!" Cassie called after her, following her up the stairs.

Back in Charleston Memorial

"Follow me please."

Peter looked up from his call with Elizabeth and seeing a middle-aged woman in white hospital attire, said, "I'll need to call you back, honey."

Peter and Stephen followed the attendant through a labyrinth of halls and doors in the emergency area to a back hall of curtains with a central nursing station. The attendant led them to a larger area to the right where Peter could see a nurse fiddling with an IV.

They were led inside and the curtains closed behind them, as the middle-aged lady who led them darted off to her next patient.

"Is this your friend?" the attending nurse asked, looking up from securing the IV.

Peter came around the side of the bed and noticed that Jacob was slightly conscious, but that he had a huge bandage on his head.

"Yes, that's him. Hello Jacob. You had us really worried."

Jacob looked at Peter and the confusion was evident on his face.

"You said his name is Jacob?"

"Yes, Jacob Younginer," Peter answered.

"Jacob Younginer, huh," The nurse stepped out of the area to relay the information and returned a short while later.

Peter tried talking to Jacob while the nurse was gone, but his attempts yielded nothing but more confused looks and some incomprehensible mumbling.

"He lives in Charleston and he's from Columbia," a doctor said to the nurse after they searched his records.

"We're trying to contact his mother now. She's his next of kin."

Any ideas how your friend got knocked on the head?"

"No, we were expecting to hear from him yesterday and when we didn't, we went searching for him," Peter replied.

Are you related to Mr. Younginger?" He asked Peter and Stephen.

"No, Just friends," Peter replied.

"We really appreciate you helping us identify him," said the doctor with a slight smile. "However, since Mr. Younginer doesn't seem to have any recollection of who he is, he won't be able to give us permission to divulge any further medical information. I'm afraid you'll have to go back to the waiting room. If his memory returns, or if his next of kin grants us permission to give you any information, we'll let you know. Miss Granger will show you the way."

At that Peter and Stephen were led back through the labyrinth.

EIGHTEEN

Back in Irmo

Alfred and Hank were left alone in the foyer after Cassie followed her mother upstairs.

Hank stood stunned, grief plastered on his face.

Alfred prayed.

At this moment, the full effects of his past actions flooded Hank's heart. What the years of Tammy's nagging couldn't do, the scene which just unfolded in front of him crashed through the protective barriers of his heart.

Was he really that selfish? Had he spent so little time considering what his family needed?

They needed much more from him than a steady paycheck and discipline. Tammy had said it all along, but only now did he really understand what she was saying.

As he and Alfred closed the front door, he could hear Tammy's sobs through the open upstairs bedroom window.

They rode along in silence for a while until Hank asked, "How do you recover from something like what I've done?"

"What do you mean?" Alfred asked.

"You saw it. You saw Tammy and Cassie, their tears. I've failed utterly as a husband and a father," Hank said. "Where can I possibly go from here?"

"You may not see it yet, but failure is often a vital step in the process."

"In the process of what; worst family man of the year?"

"No, not that," Alfred said. "People fail all the time, but it's the steps after failure which make or break a man."

"What steps are there?"

"In my opinion," Alfred began. "You can step toward God or away from him, one leads to real healing, the other can make matters worse."

"Do you think I've stepped away from God?"

"Hank. I'm not the judge of any man's heart, but without God, all a person can do is try harder in their own strength, becoming more and more driven by an ever-increasing list of duties which promise success, but produce stress, anger and burnout. It's a vicious cycle."

"I definitely understand stress, anger and burnout," Hank admitted. "But I don't understand what you mean by trying in my own strength."

"Humans were created to be Indwelled by God's Holy Spirit, to rest in his love and to love others as he's loved us. When you yield to God, you love Tammy and your kids with a love only God can give you."

"But I know plenty of people who have happy families and don't rely upon God. God can't be the only answer." Hank responded, as he merged into the highway traffic headed downtown from the exit ramp.

"True, people can have a measure of happiness without God, but there's a God sized hole in the heart of every human being. Only he can bring the joy we all long for. Money, success, popularity, even a happy family will not satisfy us for long. Without God, we'll keep seeking for something more." Alfred said, looking over at Hank as they crossed under a bridge on the interstate.

Hank said nothing for a while, then said, "Some of what you're saying makes sense. I've realized that void myself. Things I think will make me happy never really do. Tammy's experienced some of the joy you're speaking of. She's said some of the same things to me."

"If you think about it, Hank, if your failure as a husband and father can help you realize you need God, you're better off than those who're still trying to find happiness in other things," Alfred said as Hank pulled into his parking place and cut off the car.

Before they got out, Alfred continued. "If a person allows failure to do its intended work, it can lead as no words ever could. Failure as a father, a husband, a business man, a student, or just plain failure to find happiness and fulfillment brings a man over and over again to the crossroads of life. Stepping towards God is a step towards finding our joy in him, which is what he created us for."

Hank pulled the key out of the ignition and looked straight ahead in thought. After a moment he asked, "If God created us to find our joy in him, why did he create all the rest of this stuff? Was it just to tempt us?"

At that moment Hank's cell phone rang. Seeing it was Peter Anderson, he answered it.

"Hank, this is Peter. We've found Jacob. He's in the Emergency Room at Charleston Memorial."

"What the hell happened?" Hank asked.

"Looks like he's been hit on the head pretty badly, but since we aren't family, they won't tell us much."

"Do you think I should bring him this letter from Dr. Shuler?" asked Hank.

"I suppose you could. If they let you deliver it, maybe it can spur his memory. Right now I think his memory's shot. However, his mother's supposedly coming down from your way. I guess you could bring it to the hospital and try and give it to her for him."

"I might come on down now," said Hank. "But Dr. Shuler made me promise that only Jacob is to open it. So I'll have to hope to get it to him. You say Charleston Memorial?"

"That's right. Call me when you get here, we're headed back to Sarah's condo. We haven't found her yet."

"Okay; will do. Thanks." Hank replied.

Peter hung up the phone as the guard, recognizing Stephen's car, waved them clear at the Kiawah Island security gate.

As they neared Sea Forest Drive and turned toward Mariner's Watch, they began to hear the ever-increasing sound of an approaching siren. Then suddenly a dark grey Lexus squealed its tires as it turned from Sea Forest Drive and whizzed past them. Stephen pulled over and within a few seconds, the blue lights and shrill of a county deputy car erupted past them in the same direction as the Lexus.

"Somebody's going to crash if they don't slow down. They're going so fast I couldn't get even get a glimpse of who was in that car." Peter said.

"It was a man driving," Stephen said, as he shifted back into drive. "And there was a passenger, but I only saw a brief image."

"I don't feel good about this," Peter said.

Moments later, as they reached the condo, Mrs. Jenkins was standing in the driveway. When she recognized Peter, she broke down in tears.

Back in downtown Columbia

Hank looked over at Alfred, after hanging up with Peter. "Do you want to continue our conversation during a trip to Charleston?"

"Sure," Alfred said. "It would be a double blessing for me, especially if we see Peter Anderson while we're there."

"You know Professor Anderson?"

"I sure do," Alfred smiled. "We had quite an adventure together a few years ago."

"Wow. What a coincidence," Hank said, as he closed the car door.

"I don't think so," replied Alfred.

"You don't think so?" asked Hank with a quizzical look on his face. "What do you mean?"

"I don't think it's a coincidence that we both know Peter," Alfred said with a grin.

"Meet you back at the car in ten minutes," Hank said returning the grin.

NINETEEN

"I'm glad you're curious about the big picture," Alfred said as Hank merged into the traffic heading East on I-26 toward Charleston. "And I want to answer your question, but when I'm through, I'd like to ask you a question."

"Fair enough," Hank replied, happy to have a diversion to keep his mind off the mess his family was in.

"God most certainly didn't create the pleasures of life to distract us from him and to tempt us into finding our pleasures elsewhere. What God has created is the cherry and whipped cream on top, an add-on to the ice cream sundae with hot mocha chocolate fudge. As I said before, he himself is what our hearts long for, the source of all joy. What God has created for us to enjoy: sunsets, mountain ranges, flowers, puppies, chocolate pie, football and the like, even sex, in the context of marriage, was never meant to be enjoyed apart from his presence in our lives.

"We can make a meal of a bowl of whip cream with a cherry, and it would bring a bit of fleeting delight, but without the hot fudge and creamy ice cream underneath, it's hardly substantial.

"It brings God great pleasure for his children to enjoy the beauties and delicacies of this world. However, they were meant to be enjoyed as part of an intimate relationship with him."

"How do you think that applies to my situation?" Hank asked, searching to connect with what Alfred was saying.

"Hank, people naturally do life without God."

"I can agree with that," Hank said, nodding. "But ..."

"And," Alfred continued before Hank could respond. "If you think about it, with God not in the picture, men are left to formulate their own ideas concerning life's purpose and their own value."

Hank didn't say anything.

"Do you think that's true?" Alfred asked a few moments later.

"I've never wanted to be some 'born again' person who lived under a bunch of rules." Hank answered.

"I can understand that," Alfred responded.

"And I've hated the way Christians judge others," Hank said. "However, on the other hand, I don't see how a world like we live in could spring up from pond sludge. I do believe in a master designer. But I don't always agree with his ways.

"But, to your question. I have never considered relating to him when it comes to everyday choices, directions and purposes. I have pretty much felt as if it is totally up to me to take care of the details of my life."

"So, what do you think your family would say has kept your heart from them? What has competed with them for your time?"

"Work," Hank replied immediately. "I've always wanted to be successful, I hate failure. I've felt my family needed me most as a provider. So I worked hard. I'm respected at work, an exemplary employee. My family never missed a meal. They've always had clothes on their backs and a shelter over their heads."

Hank braked as he noticed the traffic ahead slowing down ahead.

"But I've never felt successful as a husband and a father," Hank continued. "Part of it has been that I just don't know how. I know how to program a computer. I went to school for that, but leading a family is a real struggle."

"Being a man, a family man, was never a job designed for you to tackle yourself," Alfred said.

"Now you tell me," Hank responded with a smile. "I think I thrive on being respected. It makes me feel valued when I succeed with a project. But at home, I don't feel respected, especially, by my son. I wanted to prepare Daniel for manhood, so I pushed him to excel. Was that wrong?"

"Encouraging excellence isn't wrong," Alfred replied. "However without awareness of love, pushing achievement leads to rebellion. Every son must first know he's loved. The recipe for success as a husband and as a father starts and ends with love."

Alfred's words produced a sick feeling and Hank felt queasy. Pushing achievement had been his first concern with Daniel. Praises from his own dad had only come when he excelled. It was all he knew. He loved Daniel, but only knew how to show it by pushing him to be the best.

Traffic slowed to a crawl as they approached Orangeburg, South Carolina. Hank inched the car forward in deep thought.

Daniel had definitely rebelled when Hank had pushed compliance. He seemed to have already known that there's more to life than achieving. Maybe he'd learned it from Tammy, Hank thought.

Alfred silently prayed that God's spirit would reveal and heal.

Traffic movement began to speed up.

After a while Alfred said, "You may be feeling a lot of regret right now. But figuring that you can't do life alone is a key part of the journey, often the hardest part. When you embrace it and surrender the mess to God, healing can begin, for you and for your family."

Hank said nothing.

"You said you had a question for me?" Hank said after a long while.

Alfred smiled. "It's not an original question. I'd like to ask you what you asked me earlier.

"Where do you go from here? What is your next step? And I'm not expecting you to answer me."

"Fair enough," Hank responded, feeling a spark of hope.

"I do have another question for you, however. You said earlier that man was created to have an intimate relationship with God and to enjoy being with him. How is that possible with someone we don't see?"

"Just talk to Him. It's really a whole lot simpler than people think. The more you talk to him, out loud and in your mind, as you go about your day, the more you become aware of his nearness.

"Eventually, you'll see finger prints. He's been around you all your life. You just didn't know how to recognize him, but you will."

Back on Kiawah Island

"What happened?" Peter said as he threw open the passenger door and approached Mrs. Jenkins.

"I called the sheriff's office about Sarah. I was answering some questions with a deputy and telling him about Matt Baston's violent behavior, when he drove up with Sarah. The deputy approached his car and he took off."

"Then, that was them we just saw. They almost flipped making that turn back there." Stephen said.

Stephen's phone rang and he walked away to answer it. When he was through with his conversation, he walked over to the condo steps where Peter was seated with Mrs. Jenkins, trying to calm her down.

"Mrs. Jenkins, I certainly hope they're able to stop that man and that your daughter is returned safely to you," Stephen said. "I need to go. Work calls."

"Thank you, Mr. Davis," Mrs. Jenkins responded.

Peter followed Stephen back to his car.

"Good news for me, bad news for you, Peter," Stephen said as he opened his car door.

"What do you mean?"

"That was Jimmy on the phone. He's done it. He sent a Morse code message back in time. We picked an exact time we knew I was star gazing while in college back in the early eighties. Sent a simple message for me to hide something in a place that's been undisturbed since then."

"What did you use?" Peter asked, remembering vaguely that he chose to tell his 12 your old self to hide baseball cards in the ceiling tiles of his childhood bedroom. When he and Jimmy found them, it proved his message was received in the past."

"I'm afraid we weren't too original. Jimmy instructed me to buy a magazine highlighting the Dodgers beating your Yankees in the 1981 World Series."

"Ouch. That's a double hurt." Peter grimaced. "Where'd you hide it?"

"In the attic of our family beach house on Sullivan's Island. I'm headed there now to see if I can find it. If I do, you know what's next."

Stephen paused for effect.

"We're going to use what we've learned how to do to help somebody, Peter. We're going to reverse a tragic event and hope we don't mess up other events by doing so."

Peter started to respond, but Stephen held up his hand. "I know you don't approve, but we'll be careful. Jimmy and I both understand the risk we're taking on by changing even a small event that has already happened."

"Well, let me know if you find the magazine." Peter said, returning back toward Mrs. Jenkins. "I'd at least like a little warning before you try this madness."

Stephen smiled, catching the not so subtle warning of impending doom. "Okay, I'll give you a call. I want to know what happens with Sarah and Jacob as well."

At Charleston Memorial

"Sarah! Sarah!"

The nurse emerged out of Jacob's room searching for Dr. Evans.

"Jacob Younginer is very agitated," she exclaimed. "His memory seems to be coming back. He told me his name and he's calling for someone named Sarah."

TWENTY

"What happened to you Mr. Younginer?" Dr. Evans asked him after they were able to settle him down with a mild sedative.

"Sarah," he said softly. "Where is Sarah? Did she get my letter?"

Jacob raised himself on his elbows and dazedly looked around.

"Sarah who?"

"Sarah Jenkins. Did she get it? Where is she?"

"Mr. Younginer, you need to lie back down. You have IVs in your arms. I'm afraid we don't know anything about the letter. You were found in a sand dune this morning on Kiawah Island. They found you with a pretty significant gash on your head, but there was no letter. In fact you had nothing, no wallet, no cell phone, nothing. Did somebody rob you?"

"Did he take the letter?" Jacob laid his head back and closed his eyes.

"Who? Did who take the letter?" Dr. Evans asked, but there was no response.

"His mother is here," an attendant announced through the curtain.

"Okay, send her to the ICU waiting room," Dr. Evans said, writing on the chart he had in his hand. "A bed just opened up."

Meanwhile downstairs

Hank and Alfred arrived at Charleston Memorial after their trip down I-26.

"We're here to see Jacob Younginer," Hank said to the emergency room attendant.

Alfred scanned the room, watching the faces of those waiting. His eyes locked on a little girl in a pink dress, with feathers, trying to control her sobbing as she held her arm, wrapped in a towel. Her mother was explaining to the man next to them that she fell on her arm during a dance recital routine.

"He's being moved to ICU on the forth floor," the attendant said to Hank after a few moments. "There's a waiting room up there. Take the elevator through that door and follow the signs."

They followed the instructions and as the elevator opened, a sterile hospital smell filled the air. Around a corner and down a long hall they followed the signs to the ICU waiting room and sat down, Hank near the door and Alfred next to an elderly lady staring blankly ahead.

After a few moments Alfred asked, "Are you here about your child?"

"Why yes, I'm here about my son," the lady exclaimed. "Though he's hardly a child anymore. How did you know? Are you a chaplain?"

"Not exactly, but I try to be aware of those around me. A mother's pain is easy to discern."

"Mrs. Younginer?" an attendant announced from the doorway. "You can see your son now." The lady stood up and glanced down at Alfred with a forced smile.

"You gentlemen will have to wait to see him," the attendant said, looking down at Alfred and Hank. "Only family for now."

"Do you know Jacob?" Mrs. Younginer asked Alfred, looking back at him as she reached the doorway.

"Not yet," Alfred replied with a smile. "But I'm looking forward to meeting him."

Between Kiawah Island and Charleston

"Slow down!" Sarah screamed. "You're going to kill us!"

They were on a long stretch of bypass heading into downtown Charleston, chased by three deputy cars.

Sarah looked behind them at the line of flashing blue lights, her fingers digging into the console. Matt bestowed a calm confidence as he accelerated to almost 110 miles per hour.

Sarah covered her eyes and prayed to a God she hoped was still there.

The sound of the sirens faded slightly as Matt slowed down to 70 mph. Sarah suddenly felt the brakes, opened her eyes and screamed.

The road they were on was ending and there was no way Matt could stop their momentum. They approached a T bone intersection at a busy commercial bypass.

Smoke filled the sky as the tires squealed and the Lexus spun around in the middle of the intersection, narrowly avoiding a pick up truck and a sedan. When the smoke cleared, they were facing the direction they were coming from, the car stalled and the blue lights were almost upon them.

"Matt, you're caught," Sarah yelled, grabbing at his arms as he turned the ignition key, restarting the car.

"No I'm not," Matt cried, angrily pushing Sarah hard against the passenger door.

Matt accelerated towards the next intersection as the sheriff's cars followed, squealing tires as they navigated the turn.

Up ahead the light turned red 100 feet before they reached the intersection. Matt did not slow down, but neither did the SUV approaching from the left.

Sarah saw it, but had little time to prepare. She tried to duck her head between her knees.

The blue SUV crushed with exploding impact into the driver side of the Lexus, sending it sideways, glass shattering, into another vehicle.

Moments later, blue lights bordered the smoking wreckage.

Back at the Jenkins Condo

"I'm going to wait with you until Sarah is rescued," Peter assured Mrs. Jenkins. They'd moved inside the condo and were sitting on the porch facing the forest path leading down to the dunes.

"Thanks Peter. I don't know what to expect. Sarah's been through such pain these last few years. How could she have gotten mixed up with a man like Matt Baston?"

Peter said nothing, but nodded in agreement.

"It's so strange that Jacob's letter never made it to her! Poor Sarah, these kind of weird happenings seem to follow her."

As Mrs. Jenkins spoke Peter thought back to his childhood days with Sarah and Benjamin; the chaos of an alcoholic, abusive father.

"Peter," Mrs. Jenkins looked at him, eyes locked. "Do you think God hates me? Why do you think all these things have happened to my children? You have kids now. Can you imagine how you would feel if you were in my shoes?"

"No I can't, Mrs. Jenkins. Thinking of harm coming to my twins is beyond comprehension. I honestly don't know how you've made it."

"I don't think I have made it, Peter. I'm coming apart." She wiped a tear with the back of her hand.

Peter spotted a tissue box on a table near the door grabbed it.

"I can't pretend to understand what you're going through," Peter said, after handing her the tissue box. But I do know one thing for certain. God doesn't hate you. In fact, as contrary as it might seem, he loves you even more than you love Sarah."

"It sure doesn't seem like it!" Mrs. Jenkins exclaimed, now sobbing.

"After Benjamin killed himself," Peter began. "I began to think God was either very weak or very cruel."

Mrs. Jenkins closed her eyes as she took in Peter's words.

"But in the years since, I have come to know God in a personal way, not just in a religious, following all the rules, kind of way. I have an actual relationship with him now. I'm learning his ways, beginning to comprehend his power and his love. I don't believe God intended for you to experience so much pain."

Mrs. Jenkins opened her eyes and looked at Peter.

"God bestowed upon man a great gift. He gave us all a free will to choose the paths of our lives. Though he longs for all of us to choose his ways, he doesn't force us. But what he does give us is Himself. He promises to see us through anything. Remember the 23rd Psalm, "Though I walk through the valley of the shadow of death, I will not fear, for you are with me.""

Mrs. Jenkins repeated the last part of the verse with Peter.

"Though it may not have seemed like it. He's been with you through it and is with us now."

Mrs. Jenkins said nothing, but after a few minutes stood and grabbed Peter's empty tea glass.

"I'm going to finish making some chicken salad for us," she said forcing a smile and leaving the porch.

While Mrs. Jenkins was in the kitchen, Peter answered a call from Stephen.

"Any word about Sarah, did the cops catch that crazy driver?"

"No word yet, but I'm still here with her mom. What's up? Did you find the magazine you planted from the 1980s?"

"Yes we did," Stephen replied, the excitement gushing through the phone. "I'm looking at it now. We are in business. As soon as we can find a situation to fix, we will send a message to myself in 1981 telling me what to do to fix a problem which has already happened by changing some key action."

"Please talk to me before you do it," Peter pleaded, hoping he could still talk them out of it.

"We'll try Peter," Stephen said. "Hey listen, I've got to go. This is Jimmy calling in."

After a few minutes, Mrs. Jenkins returned to the porch and handed Peter a refilled tea glass and a chicken salad sandwich.

"Yes!" Peter exclaimed. "I've always loved your chicken salad. This takes me back 40 years."

Mrs. Jenkins smiled and sat down.

The cool late afternoon sea breeze rushed across their faces as they stared at the forest path leading down to the dunes.

"I'm glad you were able to hang onto this place," Peter commented, popping the last of the sandwich in his mouth and washing it down with a gulp of tea.

Mrs. Jenkins smiled and nodded, but before she could respond, there was a knock at the door.

TWENTY ONE

"Mrs. Jenkins?" The deputy confirmed as she swung the door opened.

"Did you catch him?" she asked anxiously, instantly noticing the officer's somber expression.

"Matt Baston is dead, Mrs. Jenkins. He ran a red light during the chase and the car he and your daughter were in was crushed by an SUV at an intersection. But your daughter is alive."

The officer paused a moment before continuing. "I'm afraid she's been hurt severely, ma'am. I'm here to drive you to Charleston Memorial."

All the color rushed out of Mrs. Jenkins face as she looked over her shoulder at Peter standing behind her.

"Peter!" she cried out.

"Go with him," Peter urged. "I saw your keys on the dining room table. I'll lock up and meet you there."

With that the deputy escorted her to his car and Peter saw them blaze away, blue lights flashing.

As he gathered Mrs. Jenkin's keys, he paused and stared through the porch door to the forest path down to the beach beyond.

How could this be happening?

Back at Charleston Memorial

"One of you can see Jacob Younginer now," the attendant said to Hank and Alfred as she appeared in the doorway of the waiting room. "Mrs. Younginer is still in there and the maximum number of visitors at a time is two."

Hank stood up and checked his upper pocket to be sure Dr. Shuler's letter was still there. He looked down at Alfred and said, "Wish me luck."

"I'll do more than that," the elderly black man said with a smile.

By now, Hank knew what his new friend meant.

Hank followed the attendant and entered the room. He was surprised to see the bed slightly raised and Jacob talking with his mother.

Jacob looked at the door when Hank came in, searching his mind for who he was.

Hank picked up on it and introduced himself. "Hello Jacob. I'm Hank Eagan, Cassie and Daniel's father. We missed each other yesterday when you came by the house."

"Yeah, okay," Jacob said slowly. "You went with Cassie to deliver my letter to Sarah. Thank you for trying. I'm afraid I didn't have much luck delivering it either.

"I heard," Hank replied. "But I'm glad to see you awake.

"I'm feeling a bit better. Thank you for coming all this way to check on me."

Jacob paused a moment then said, "Hank, this is my mother, Betty Younginer."

"Hello, Mrs. Younginer," Hank said extending his hand. "We saw you in the waiting room a little while ago,"

"Yes," she said. "Please call me Betty. You were with the black gentleman I sat next to?"

"Yes. His name is Alfred. He's my neighbor back in Columbia."

"Did your son show up?" Jacob asked.

"Yes he did," Hank said, happy to see Jacob in such a sound mind. "Seems he was kidnapped, but he made it through the ordeal."

"Oh my," Betty gasped. "Kidnapped? Did they catch who did it?"

"They think they know who did it, but they haven't arrested him down yet. But I'm confident they'll catch him soon."

"That's disconcerting," Betty replied. "I'm sure it's tough for you to be here, knowing your son's kidnapper is still at large."

Her comment took Hank aback. He honestly hadn't thought of it that way. He felt ashamed.

"Yes Ma'am," he stuttered. "But I came to deliver something to Jacob that seemed pretty urgent," He reached in his top pocket and grabbed the letter.

"Jacob," Hank said, moving around the bed and sitting in a chair by the curtain that separated Jacob from the other ICU patients. "This morning Daniel and I took your other undelivered letter to Dr. Shuler."

"Undelivered letter?" Betty questioned. "What letter?"

"Yea, mom; a couple of my letters I wrote three years ago were never delivered. Sarah never got my letter either," Jacob said, with slurred, but passionate words, his eyes beginning to close to half mast.

"What about Dr. Shuler? How do you know him?" Betty asked, seemingly ignoring what Jacob said about his letter to Sarah.

"I haven't had a chance to tell you about it mom," Jacob said slowly, exaggerating every syllable. "I found a really nasty note in Pop Younginer's attic. It was from his brother Luke."

Jacob closed his eyes then continued very slowly. "It mentioned some crusade against the Hope family. And there was a map to a grave y….."

Jacob nodded and then closed his eyes again, this time they didn't open.

"Expect him to be in and out for a while," said the nurse as she lowered the light. "He needs to rest. He's on some pretty powerful sedatives. I'll be back to check on him soon."

"Why were the letters undelivered?" Betty asked Hank softly, as the nurse left.

"We don't know, but my children found two of your son's letters and opened them both," Hank replied. "From a phone number in one of the letters, my daughter contacted your son. His letter to Sarah touched her deeply and she's been determined for Sarah to get it. As you can imagine, Jacob was dumbfounded to realize that neither of his letters were delivered. He seemed particularly intent on getting his letter to Sarah."

"Yes," Betty broke in. "I've tried to urge him to move on after she turned him down when he asked her to marry him. But she must have had a very deep hold on his heart."

"That's just it," Hank exclaimed. "The letter that wasn't delivered was an apology and an informal marriage proposal."

"Oh my! So, she never even got his proposal?"

"No," Hank said, pausing to replay the events in his mind. "Cassie and I tried to deliver his letter to Sarah because it was addressed to a house the next street over from where we live. That's when we heard about Peter Anderson."

"Peter Anderson?"

"Yes, one of Sarah's long-time friends," Hank continued. "Sarah's moved and Peter knew where she was here in Charleston, well actually on Kiawah Island."

"Seems Jacob did mention Sarah's family has a condo there," Betty recalled.

"Yes, and yesterday, Jacob set out to the Island to deliver his letter to Sarah."

"And that's how he ended up here," Betty completed the thought.

"Yes, I guess so," Hank agreed. "They don't know what happened to him?"

"No, not really" Betty replied. "He's screamed some things about Sarah, but he's been fading in and out of lucidness."

After a while, Jacob groaned softly and his eyes opened and closed halfway, then shut again.

In a few more minutes Jacob seemed to be almost fully awake so Hank seized the opportunity and said, "Jacob, my son, Daniel, and I delivered your letter to Dr. Shuler this morning. And in turn, he asked me to deliver this letter to you."

Hank held the letter up.

"Do you mind if I see it?" asked Betty.

"Well," Hank paused. "Dr. Shuler told me to be sure I delivered it only to Jacob."

"I see," Betty said.

At that, Dr. Evans entered the room to check on Jacob.

"I need some air," Betty said as Dr. Evans began looking at Jacob's chart. "Do you want me to send your friend in?"

"Yes, please," replied Hank.

A few moments later, Alfred entered the room as Dr. Evans was leaving. Jacob appeared lucid and a dinner tray was brought in.

"You gentlemen can stay for a little while longer," a nurse said. "After Mr. Younginer finishes eating, we need to get him ready for the night."

"Will do," said Hank, turning his attention to Jacob. "Jacob, this is my neighbor, Alfred. I just recently met him, but he's been a real solace to me during my family distress."

"Nice to meet you, Alfred," responded Jacob as he slurped a spoon full of soup. "I hate to eat in front of you, but I finally feel like eating and need to get something in my stomach."

"No problem," Hank replied, anxious to complete his mission. "Jacob, as I was saying earlier, I delivered your letter to Dr. Shuler and he gave me a letter to give you. It's from his mother."

Hank handed him the letter and Jacob put down his fork and grabbed it. He opened it with the butter knife on his tray and began reading.

As he read, Jacob's lips tightened and slightly shifted.

Alfred and Hank watched his eyes scan the page. Jacob then folded the letter and put it back in the envelope. He laid the letter beside his bed and stared ahead, fighting his emotions. To Alfred and Hank he looked both angry and sad.

"Hank, is my mother still here?"

"She stepped outside for some air," Hank replied.

"Would you please go find her and ask her to come here?"

"Sure Jacob. Is everything okay?"

"Evidently I'm adopted."

Meanwhile downstairs

The deputy turned his blue lights off and opened the door for Mrs. Jenkins at the emergency room entrance to Charleston Memorial.

She walked slowly through the doors as they automatically opened.

When she announced herself at the front desk, she was directed to the elevators and to the sixth floor waiting room. Checking in at the nurse's station, she was told that

Sarah was in surgery and that the surgeon would update her as soon as possible.

As Peter was pulling into a parking place in the emergency room area, his phone rang. It was Tammy.

"Professor Anderson," she said excitedly. "Do you know where Hank is? I've tried to call him, but he's not picking up."

"Yes, he's down here in Charleston, at the hospital delivering a letter to Jacob Younginer. Is everything all right?"

"Cassie was playing in the back yard near the barn and saw a man peering at her from the woods. We're afraid it could be the man who kidnapped Daniel."

"Did you call the Sheriff's department?"

"I just did, but I would like to talk to Hank. If you see him, would you tell him to call me?"

"I sure will, Tammy. I'm at the hospital now. I'm sure I'll see him soon. Hang in there."

"I'm trying," she replied.

Peter hung up and as he approached the Emergency room doors, they opened and Hank and Alfred emerged.

TWENTY TWO

"Alfred!" Peter exclaimed. "What are you doing here?"

"I heard you were trying to have an adventure without me," Alfred said, smiling.

When Peter cracked a slight grin, Alfred added. "Hank's my neighbor. His condo is right around the corner from mine."

"What's wrong Peter?" asked Hank, picking up on his solemn expression.

"I'll fill you in soon," Peter replied, "but first, Hank, you need to call Tammy. We'll wait here for you."

"Is she okay?"

"She needs to talk to you," Peter urged.

Hank pulled out his cell phone and dialed Tammy's number, walking toward his car as the phone rang.

Alfred spotted Betty Younginer sitting on an outside bench, lighting a new cigarette from the one she had in her hand.

"Excuse me a moment, Peter," Alfred said. "I have a message to deliver. I'll be right back."

At that, Alfred walked over to where Betty was nervously puffing away. Peter could see him telling her something. Then he saw her eyes widen as she slowly stood up. She then dropped her cigarette, stepped on it and ambled toward the automatic doors, passing in front of Peter.

"That was Jacob's mother," Alfred explained. "He's doing better. At least he was until Hank gave him the letter from Dr. Shuler. Seems he and his mom have a lot to talk about."

Peter nodded a response and then looked gravely into the kind dark eyes of his old friend. "Sarah's been hurt really badly, Alfred." Peter exclaimed. "She's still alive, but in critical condition. I was with her mom when she found out. She's already here. I need to go be with her as soon as I can."

"You go on," Alfred urged. "I'll wait for Hank and let him know where you are."

"I hope Hank decides to go home to his family," said Peter. "They need him right now."

"I know," responded Alfred. "Peter, if Hank does go back now, may I ride back to Columbia with you?"

Peter smiled. "I would love it, but what about Hank. Doesn't he need you?"

"Not if he makes the right choice and decides to go home," Alfred replied.

Peter nodded and disappeared through the automatic doors.

Back in Irmo

Tammy's cell phone rang. Seeing Hank's name on the caller ID, she quickly answered.

"Please come home, Hank."

"Sure I will, honey," Hank replied, surprising himself as well as Tammy with such endearing words. "What's wrong?"

"Peter Anderson didn't tell you?"

"No, he just told me to call you. What's going on?"

"Cassie saw a man in the woods and she thinks it's the same man that kidnapped Daniel!" Tammy exclaimed hysterically.

"Call the Sheriff!" Hank exclaimed. "I'm on my way."

Hank hung up the phone and jogged back to where Peter and Alfred were. Only Alfred remained.

"Alfred, we need to head on back. Tammy needs me."

"Unless you need me, Hank," Alfred replied. "I'd like to stay here. Sarah has been in a severe accident and I think Peter could use my help. He said I can ride back to Columbia with him."

"That's fine, Alfred. Is Sarah going to be all right?" Hank called back, now jogging back toward his car.

"I don't know," Alfred replied. "I pray so."

Alfred stopped by the emergency room desk and followed their directions to the waiting room where he found Mrs. Jenkins and Peter. They were the only ones in the room. She was sobbing and Peter was consoling her.

"All her hopes and dreams!" she cried. "Why is all this happening to my little girl?"

"They finished operating on Sarah," Peter said, looking up at Alfred.

"She's paralyzed!" Mrs. Jenkins cried out. "They're not sure she'll make it through the night. Why Peter? People have been so cruel to my Sarah her whole life; her father, the people in the mental hospital and now this Matt Baston fiend."

Peter looked up at Alfred as if to say, this one's yours.

He picked up on it and came around on the other side of Mrs. Jenkins and sat down.

"I feel like I know you, Mrs. Jenkins," he began. "My name is Alfred and I'm a friend of Peter and Sarah's. I actually met Sarah a number of years ago when my wife, Susan and I volunteered at the state mental hospital on Bull Street."

Mrs. Jenkins looked over at the warm coffee-colored eyes of the stately gentleman and wiped a tear. "You can call me Alice if you'd like. You knew Sarah back then?"

"I did," continued Alfred. "And I want you to know that even in my brief encounters with her, she mentioned how much she loves you and how having a mother like you, who loves her so unconditionally, has been what's kept her alive."

"She said that?" Alice asked as she erupted into hysterics again.

Peter tried to comfort her by rubbing her shoulder.

"I wasn't there for either of my children when they were growing up," She said between sobs. "I was so worried about surviving their father's alcoholism that I didn't have anything left for them!"

"Sarah has always known you love her. In spite of how you think you failed her," Peter replied. "Children know when they're loved. It can't be hidden when it is real. Sincere love makes up for a lot of mistakes.

"Being a parent isn't easy. My twins are approaching four years old and they keep me on my knees."

Alice let their words of consolation settle and closed her eyes.

Back in Irmo

"Is Daddy coming?" Cassie asked when Tammy hung up the phone.

"Yes, he's on his way?" Tammy replied.

"How long will it take for him to get here?" Daniel asked.

"He's coming from Charleston, so a couple of hours," Tammy answered, somewhat surprised by Daniel's interest in his father's whereabouts.

Suddenly, there was a knock at the door.

"Finally," Tammy said, approaching the door.

"Who is it Momma? Cassie asked.

"The sheriff's deputy I certainly hope," answered Tammy.

"Mrs. Eagan?" asked a voice from the other side of the door."

"It's him!" Daniel whispered urgently as he grabbed his mother's arm. "That's the man that kidnapped me. It's him!"

Cassie screamed.

TWENTY THREE

What happened next couldn't have been predicted. Bubba hadn't come to harass, but to apologize.

"We've called the sheriffs," Tammy screamed. "Leave us alone!"

"I've come to give up," Bubba said through the closed door. "I can't believe I actually kidnapped your boy. I'm sorry."

"It's a trick," Daniel said in a loud whisper. "Just ignore him."

"But Cassie asked, "Why'd you do it?"

What came out of Bubba's mouth next was the result of his dark night of the soul. A night hidden away in the darkness of the woods as he heard the voices of those chasing him; saw their flashlights, heard the hounds. He'd traveled along the creek bed, hoping his scent had been covered.

When the lights snuffed out one by one and the noises faded, he was left alone; totally alone. He knew that if there was a God, then God was all he had. He was utterly, helplessly alone. In the darkness of a moonless night behind a thicket of trees, in a bed of leaves and spiky gum balls, he searched for forgiveness.

He was at a crossroad. He could choose despair, which was the choice he'd always made; feeling sorry for himself; loathing his slowness of mind and slothfulness. Food and beer had always numbed the pain, at least for a while. But each time he woke up empty and angry, thinking only of how to start the cycle again.

Just before sun rise he made a different choice. He cried out to a God he wasn't really sure was even there; asking for forgiveness, for a path out of the pit. As the first pin holes of light began to break through the forest, he determined to turn himself in.

As the sun broke fully through the low hanging limbs in the deepness of his forest hideaway, he again walked along the creek bed, this time in the other direction, toward the Eagan house. He crossed the road and entered another part of the woods across from their house. There he waited most of the day. He needed to ask for forgiveness.

"I was desperate," he replied to Cassie's question. "MB gave me beer and money for food, so I did what he asked me to do. Before I knew it, I was doing things I would never do in my right mind."

"Don't believe him," Daniel said. "He's trying to get us to open the door."

"I don't blame you for not trusting me," Bubba replied, as he began to hear the ever-increasing sound of approaching sirens. "I'm here to give myself up, but I wanted to say I'm sorry to you first. I know I caused your whole family a whole lot of pain."

"That doesn't solve a thing," Daniel yelled.

"I know," Bubba said as three deputy cars pulled into the Eagan drive way, lights flashing. "But I needed to say it anyway."

Back at Charleston Memorial

With mounting dread, Betty Younginer exited the elevator and slowly ambled past the nursing station toward Jacob's room. In her heart she knew what Dr. Shuler's letter must have said and now she had to try and explain the deception to her son.

When she entered the room, Jacob had once again dozed off. She quietly sat in the chair next to the window. Jacob discerned the movement and opened his eyes.

Betty expected her son to be angry at her, but instead he appeared hurt.

"Mom," Jacob began, his lips slightly trembling. "Tell me about this letter. Dr. Shuler says you adopted me. Is it true?"

"I'm afraid it is son. Your father and I weren't able to have children. We were presented with the possibility of adopting you and you fulfilled our dreams of having a son."

"But why didn't you tell me? Why did my real parents not want me?"

"I really don't know the whole story son, but I'll tell you what I know," Betty began. "The reason we didn't tell you is that your father doesn't know all the details of your adoption, and your real mother only approved of the adoption under the condition that I tell no one of your true origin. If I told you, you would ask questions I couldn't answer."

"But why?"

"I'm afraid the documents you found in Pop Younginer's attic were just the tip of the iceberg as to what has gone on in your father's family," she said. "He's shared very little with me and I really do think he's tried to distance himself as far as he can from his family's twisted past.

"Not that all your father's family is bad, mind you."

"Was he involved?"

"You know your father and I aren't on the best of terms these days, but I don't think he's been involved. As you know, we've had very little contact with your father's side of the family. I think I've only met his brother, your Uncle Billy, twice, once at our wedding."

"But did my real parents give me up?" Jacob asked. "Didn't they care about me?"

Betty looked away, but Jacob pressed her. "Mom, tell me what you know."

Betty paused and then walked over to Jacob's bed.

"Son, I'm sure you've probably put the pieces together by now. You're a Hope. And from what I'm told, the only Hope remaining in this area. Your parents loved you dearly, Jacob, though your biological father never laid eyes on you. He died before you were born. And your mother, Annie Hope, died in birthing you. Dr. Shuler's mother is your aunt and she arranged for you to be adopted into a family who is somehow involved in the terrible plot you read about in Pop Younginer's attic. You're like Moses, secretly adopted into a family who meant to harm you."

"Mom, I can't believe it!" Jacob said, pushing himself up on his hands in the bed.

"Settle down, son. You'll pull the IVs out of your arms."

"But I'm not your son," Jacob replied. "Do you know how hard that is to hear? To believe your whole life that your mom loved you and to all of a sudden find out that you're not my mother. How would you feel?"

"Jacob, just because I'm not your biological mother, doesn't mean I love you any less. I don't know if there is any way I could love you any more than I do. I'm very serious."

Betty took hold of Jacob's hand as she spoke. She leaned over and kissed him on the cheek.

Jacob stared ahead, trying to take in the gravity of the news.

"So, I'm a Hope?"

"Your father and I adopted you, so technically you are a Younginer."

"Does Dad know?"

"He knows you're adopted, but that's it. He doesn't know you're a Hope."

TWENTY FOUR

"Mrs. Jenkins?"

"Yes," Alice looked up at the nurse who had entered the waiting area.

"Doctor Coulter would like to talk with you in the conference room."

"May my friends join me?" she asked looking at Peter and then Alfred.

"Yes, of course," the nurse replied.

The three silently followed the nurse down the hall and into a small room with chairs lined along the wall.

"Wait here. Dr. Coulter will be with you shortly," the nurse said shutting the door behind her.

"Peter, there's something I haven't told you," Alice said as they sat down.

Peter looked over at her but kept silent.

"Sarah has a son," she said. "She's kept him hidden with me. He's three years old."

"Wow!" Peter said, looking over at Alfred and then back at Alice. "Sarah never told me about him. I'm surprised, but it makes sense now. Sarah didn't return our calls for months when she first moved to Columbia."

"She didn't tell anyone but me," Alice said. "She could never shake her love for Jacob. She was so hurt that he never contacted her; part of her hated him. However, at the same time, she had given her heart to him and she couldn't get it back. She loves her son, but he reminds her so much of Jacob that she can only be with him in short spurts. The pain is too great."

"Elizabeth and I did notice the emptiness in her life. It broke our hearts. She's been through so much. She didn't talk about Jacob, so we didn't know that's what it was," replied Peter.

"She is so very vulnerable. I don't know how Matt Baston weaseled his way into her life, but he's totally evil. I shuttered to be around him. I know this is bad to say, but I'm happy he's dead. I just hope she can survive. Now that we know Jacob feels the same about her, their lives could be so happy."

"What's her son's name? Alfred asked.

"His name is Bryan. Bryan Benjamin Jenkins."

"I guess technically his name is Younginer, right?" Peter asked.

"I don't know how that works?" Alice replied, since they never married.

"Where is Bryan now?" asked Peter.

"He's with my sister in Greenville," Alice replied. "I came down here to try and convince Sarah to come live with me for a while. Bryan is missing her terribly."

"Mrs. Jenkins?"

"Yes." Alice said as Dr. Coulter entered the room.

"I'm Dr. Coulter."

"I'm afraid I have some very hard news for you," Dr. Coulter said in grave tones. "Your daughter Sarah is dead. The trauma to her brain was too severe. Her heart stopped beating about 15 minutes ago. We tried to revive her repeatedly, but we failed.

I'm so sorry."

"Nooooooooooooooooooo," Alice screamed. "It's not true! Peter! It can't be true!"

Peter rushed to her and held her. She moaned and sobbed loudly for as long a time as Peter held her tight. Time passed in a dream sequence until no tears remained.

Alice was in no condition to make any decisions, so Peter handled selecting a mortuary to pick up Sarah's body.

"How are you doing?" Peter asked over the phone to his wife, Elizabeth, as Alfred was talking to Alice.

"I'm okay. I'm looking forward to seeing you tomorrow. Two almost four year olds are a bit much. I'm glad both my parents are still active."

"Your parents are great," Peter said, mustering his strength. "Listen, Honey, I have some hard news for you. Sarah didn't survive the car crash. Her heart just stopped beating about an hour ago and they couldn't get it started again. The trauma to the brain from the wreck was too severe."

"Oh no; Peter, I can't believe it. I'm so sorry!"

There was silence for a while as Elizabeth absorbed the news.

"Alfred and I are with Mrs. Jenkins now. I can't even imagine the pain she's feeling."

When Elizabeth could speak again, she urged Peter to stay with Mrs. Jenkins and help as much as he could.

I'll stay with Mom and Dad if I need to," she said.

"Thanks,' Peter replied. "I think Alfred and I could be of great help down here."

Back in Irmo

There was no mercy shown toward Bubba when the deputies surrounded him in front of the Eagan's house. He was ordered to freeze and was wrestled to the ground.

He offered no resistance.

A little while after Bubba was apprehended and the sheriff's car disappeared down the lane, Hank pulled up in front of his house.

He went around to the side and entered the mud room through the garage. "Is everybody okay?" he asked as he approached the great room through the kitchen.

"Daddy!" Cassie screamed, running into his arms. He picked her up and carried her to where Tammy and Daniel were sitting, in chairs on opposite sides of the fire place.

"Too late," Daniel sneered. "The guy who kidnapped me was here at our door trying to trick us into opening it."

"He said he was sorry," Cassie said.

"Saying you're sorry hardly makes up for what he did," Daniel said.

"No, but it's a start," Hank said, as he and Cassie plopped down on the couch in front of the fire place.

"How are Sarah and Jacob?" Cassie asked eagerly.

"Both of them were in accidents," Hank said, looking over and catching Tammy's eye.

Jacob seems to be recovering, but Sarah was in a bad car wreck."

"Oh no!" Tammy said. "Is she going to be okay?"

"I really don't know? Peter Anderson is still at the hospital, we can call him later to see if there's an update. I'm afraid it was a very serious collision. The man who was driving was thrown from the car and is dead."

"Can we call Mr. Anderson to see if she's okay and see if Jacob has talked to her about how he feels?'

"Sure we can, Sweetie," Hank answered. "But I need to say a few things to all of you first."

I've been doing a whole lot of soul searching the last few days," Hank began. "And I've discovered some things about myself that have been ugly and very hard to accept."

Tammy swallowed hard, hoping and praying that this was not the beginning of another empty apology.

"I need to say something to all of you." Out of the corner of his eye, Hank saw Daniel roll his eyes, but continued. "I know I've tried to say I'm sorry before, but I'm praying, yes praying you will receive the sincerity of my words."

Hank paused and looked directly at Tammy. "I have failed our family. I haven't been the protector, the loving husband and father or the leader you've needed. I thought being a good provider was the best thing I could do for you, but I was wrong."

Hank paused a moment, as he felt pangs of emotion.

"My job kept me busy and distracted. When you needed me, I wasn't there. I was so stressed, I treated you all as obstacles to getting things done and I know you felt it.

"I know you tried to understand, at least at first, but as time went on you'll felt my absence. The distance between us grew and that just fed my growing sense of failure.

"But when this happened, I blamed you. I couldn't bear to add failure as a husband and father to the failures as a person and as a man I already felt."

Hank looked over at Tammy. "I don't understand how I didn't see what I was doing to our family and to each of you."

From Tammy, Hank looked at Cassie and finally to Daniel, who was now looking down.

"What made you realize all this?" Tammy asked.

"I guess when Daniel came up missing. Well, maybe just before that. I met Alfred the same day and he asked me some very thought-provoking questions right before you called to tell me about Daniel. Questions that made me mad at first, but questions that helped me begin to see what I was doing to you guys. And he also helped me understand about forgiveness.

"As the seriousness of your ordeal mounted," Hank now looked over at Daniel who raised his head and looked at him, "I missed you and thought I'd never see you again. I realized then that I probably hurt you most of all. I wanted you to be like me and when you wouldn't, I resented it.

"Then I felt the separation more and more and I got angry. Though I know you felt I was angry at you, I was really angry at myself for being such a horrible husband and father. It was crippling to me. I couldn't handle it. Our relationship became more about how I felt than about how I was hurting you."

Hank stood up and walked over to where Daniel was sitting and looked him in the eyes. "Son, I'm so very sorry for the way I've treated you. I'm sorry for trying to use you to make me feel good about myself. I'm sorry for trying to force you into being someone you aren't, just to make me feel good. I'm sorry for blaming you for the distance between us. You're such an amazing young man and I pray you will forgive me. I love you so very much."

Daniel's head was now in his hands and he was sobbing.

Hank put his hand on Daniel's shoulder and looked up at Tammy who was wiping a tear.

TWENTY FIVE

As Hank moved away from a still drooping Daniel, Tammy slowly approached him.

"I've never heard you talk like this, Hank," she said, gently laying her hand on his arm. "I have no doubt whatsoever about your sincerity. I really appreciate what you've said."

"But do you accept my apology? Do you forgive me?" Hank said, looking down and then into her eyes.

"Pastor Bob spoke about forgiveness this past Sunday. Didn't he kids?" she asked.

Cassie smiled and nodded, still trying to take in the scene unfolding in front of her.

Daniel remained head down with no response.

"He preached from Matthew 18," Tammy continued, "the passage about the slave who was forgiven a fortune. He owed ten thousand talents. Pastor Bob was explaining how each talent represented a year's wages, so he owed millions upon millions of dollars."

"Wow, its hard to imagine how someone could spend that much, let alone be that much in debt," Hank commented. "If I owed that much, I couldn't bear up under the weight. Debt feels like walking around under a cold wet blanket."

"Yes; that much debt is unimaginable, a sum impossible to pay back. That was the point, Pastor Bob said. The slave represents us and the impossible debt we owe for our sins, even if we offered our lives, it wouldn't pay it. Only a life lived perfectly could satisfy our debt. That's what made Christ's willingness to die in our place so unimaginable and critical; a perfect man dying to pay a debt we couldn't pay."

"I hadn't thought about it that way," replied Hank, sitting back down to take in what Tammy was saying. "When you put what Jesus did on the cross in terms of paying our debt, it makes it much easier to understand."

There was silence in the room for a good while. Tammy sat back down and Hank appeared to be in deep thought.

"Do you remember what the slave who owed all that money did after his lord forgave him?" Tammy asked, looking at Hank.

"No, not really," he answered.

"Well when his lord forgave him, he went right out and found a fellow who owed him a small fraction of what he owed, less than a thousand, and began choking him and demanding it be paid back. His fellow slave begged for mercy, but he was unwilling to forgive him and threw him in jail. When his lord found out what he had done with his fellow slave, he was turned over to be tortured until he could pay back his millions."

Tammy stood up and walked over to where Hank was sitting. "Hank, I do believe you're sincere in your apology. And me not forgiving you after all that God has forgiven me for, would be no less grievous than what this slave did after his lord forgave his millions and millions.

"Hank, I do forgive you."

"What does this mean about us?" Hank asked. "Do we have a chance? I'd love to come back, if you'd have me."

Tammy smiled. "I said I forgive you. You'll have to give me some time on the other."

She squeezed his hand and sat back down.

"Fair enough," Hank replied. "But just know I'm all in, Tammy. I'm very sorry I left and if and when you're ready, it would be my privilege to spend the rest of my life with you and the kids."

Tammy slowly wiped a tear with her index finger, but did not respond.

"Can we call Peter Anderson now?" Cassie asked, trying to wait as long as she could.

Hank and Tammy looked at each other and smiled and then Hank said, "Sure we can."

He pulled out his cell phone and dialed Peter's number.

Back at Charleston Memorial, Peter felt his phone vibrate, but didn't even look to see who it was. What he and Alfred and Mrs. Jenkins were about to do, was too important.

"May we all three go in to see Jacob Younginer?" Peter asked the attendant and the nursing station. "It's really important."

"I'd like to let you," she responded, but one of you will need to wait in the waiting room."

The attendant pointed to her right where the waiting room was, down the hall they had just traveled.

"I'll wait," Alfred offered.

He proceeded down the hall, but then turned and said to Peter, "I'll pray for you all, for the Lord's comforting presence in the midst. He is an ever present help in trouble."

"Thank you," Peter replied as he took Mrs. Jenkins arm and led her toward Jacob's room.

"Peter, I'm alone now? No husband and now both my children are dead. If it wasn't for little Bryan, I'd be all alone in this world."

"Are you worried about losing him to Jacob?" Peter asked.

Alice Jenkins bowed her head and squeezed Peter's arm, but said nothing.

After a few moments, the two entered Jacob's room and found him resting.

They sat down quietly until he opened his eyes and noticed them.

"Mrs. Jenkins!" he responded in the most enthusiastic tone he could muster. "Where is Sarah?"

Peter looked over at Alice Jenkins' watered eyes, then turned to Jacob and began. "Jacob, before we speak of Sarah, there's something you need to know."

Jacob combed both of their faces for a hint of what it was.

"During the time you and Sarah were together, you became a father."

"But she said she was on contraceptives," Jacob responded, looking embarrassingly at his mother who shook her head.

"His name is Bryan Benjamin," Peter said, purposely leaving off a last name. "You're his father."

Jacob could find no words. He stared ahead taking in the news.

"He is an absolute delight," responded Alice Jenkins with a slight smile. "He's been with me these three years."

"Why didn't she tell me?" Jacob finally asked.

"She didn't want you to be with her out of pity or obligation," Alice said. "And since she never got your letter of apology, she figured you'd moved on; though she never stopped loving you."

"Nor did I stop loving her!" Jacob said with growing excitement. "I can't wait to tell her. When can I see her?"

Jacob's heart sank as soon as he asked, seeing the sunken faces of his visitors.

"Jacob," Peter said. "Sarah died in a car accident a few hours ago."

Jacob screamed in his head, but no words came. To all who viewed him he was non-responsive for many moments.

After a while, a nurse came to attend him.

"Is everything okay in here?" she asked.

"He just found out his girlfriend and the mother of his baby is dead," Peter told her. "What!" the nurse responded in agitation. "He can't handle news like that. I'm afraid you'll have to leave."

Peter and Alice left his room and walked slowly down to where Alfred was waiting. If it was at all possible, they now felt even worse than they had before they went in.

In relative silence, Peter drove them all back to Mrs. Jenkins condo on Kiawah Island.

When they arrived, Peter helped Mrs. Jenkins work through the details of transferring Sarah's body from the local mortuary to one in Greenville where Sarah would be buried next to her brother.

With the arrangements being made, Alice began packing to return to the upstate.

"Do you think Jacob will be taking over custody of Bryan?' Alice asked.

"If he's able," Peter surmised. "However, based on his condition when we left, I'd say it may be awhile."

Alice nodded as she continued her packing.

"I think Alfred and I will drop back by the hospital on our way home to Columbia. Hopefully by then we can get a feel for how he is. If they let us see him, that is."

They said goodbye to her and left for the hospital.

Alfred and Peter traveled in silence along the long corridor of angel oak trees heading toward John's Island. With the convertible top down, the warm salty sea breeze rolled in rhythm across Peter's bald head. Deep in thought, he wondered about the pain Alice Jenkins was feeling, having now lost all of her children.

As they left the island, Peter's thoughts turned to Jacob and what he must be going through; finding out in the same day that he's a father and that the love of his life is dead.

"How do you comprehend such pain, Alfred?" Peter asked. "What do you say, how can you console?"

Alfred didn't answer immediately, but after a little while he replied. "Peter, a while back I sat down and read all 150 Psalms in 2 days. I wanted to get the essence of the whole book. Like no other scripture, I think the Psalms get to the heart of human emotion. I was fresh off losing Susan and my heart was nothing but one big strawberry."

Alfred paused a moment, fighting back a wave of emotion.

"When I read Psalm 150 and closed my Bible, God showed me a common theme, I'll never forget. In the Psalms, men are going through extreme dangers and nights of weeping. David was even so low he drooled on his beard, faking insanity to save his life. But you know, Peter, every Psalm didn't end with the circumstance necessarily changing. However, what I noticed was God's greatness and nearness proclaimed. And then as I thought about it I realized that's the message of the whole Bible, Emmanuel, God with us.

"And what greater message can we proclaim to anyone, no matter what they're going through? God never promised all our circumstances would work out, but though we walk through the valley of the shadow of death, we will not fear. Why?"

Alfred looked at Peter for the answer.

"Because God is with us," Peter answered.

"Amen," Alfred said with a smile. "And that is the message we're to carry to Jacob. We don't need to worry about how to unpack it. God will show us step by step. The only important thing for any of us is God's presence. He Himself is what we've been longing for all our lives. In His presence is fullness of joy. He is our great reward."

With renewed courage, Peter parked the car, closed the top on his convertible and they headed to Jacob's room.

TWENTY SIX

Alfred and Peter slowly opened the door to Jacob's room. It looked like he was resting, so they slipped quietly into the chairs beside his bed.

After a while a nurse came in to check on him.

"I'm afraid I'm going to have to ask you gentlemen to leave," she said. "Mr. Younginer is not doing well right now. He needs to rest."

"Is he going to be alright?" Peter asked, as he and Alfred stood up to leave.

"We certainly hope so," she replied.

Several days passed and Jacob slowly improved physically. As he lay in bed, his thoughts swirled around all he'd been told. He couldn't seem to focus. Did Sarah's mother tell him he had a son? And did his own mother tell him that he was adopted, that in fact he was a Hope? He thought about these things, but remained outwardly unresponsive.

"He's not there," a doctor commented to the nurse as Jacob was examined. "Physically, he's improving, but mentally he's retreated into shadow land."

The nurse shook her head. "You've been reading too much Lord of the Rings. Everything doesn't relate to the movie."

Chuckling, the doctor turned away without replying.

Back in the Midlands of South Carolina

Not wanting to push reconciliation on Tammy, Hank spent several nights at his condo in downtown Columbia. Though his heart now ached for his family, he realized that he had to do the work of earning their trust and proving that his love for them was sincere.

"What do you mean that you need to prove your love is sincere?" Alfred asked him a couple of days after he and Peter returned from Charleston. He and Hank were sitting on a bench outside their condos overlooking the fountain and enjoying the beginnings of a Carolina sunset.

"I've realized something pretty important," Hank answered. "I was trying to suck my value from my family. I loved them, but it was a selfish kind of love. I wanted success more than anything; to be looked at as a good business man, husband and father. But when things went wrong in any of those areas, an inner turbulence brewed which caused me to try harder not to fail. My heart was detached from those I loved and my anger began to erupt towards them."

"What changed all that?" Alfred asked.

"The conversations we've had," began Hank. "Your words about forgiveness and the way you helped me understand that a relationship with God is not based on my successes and failures, but on what Jesus did for me."

Alfred nodded.

"When I really think about the fact that I can't earn God's approval, a kind of peace comes over me. I still don't understand how the commands in the Bible fit in, but I'm sure I'll understand in time," Hank continued.

"Yes, the commands we read in the Bible can be confusing," Alfred said. "However, there's a simple way to look at them. First remember there is a reason God commanded those things for us. They represent a pattern of life which, when followed, gives us the highest chance to live a life of enjoyment in God. Regardless of how we see God and our relationship with Him, He has our best interest in mind. He created us for joy, but that joy only finds it's fullness as we enjoy Him. So, following his commandments is what's best for us, but there's a catch."

"A catch?"

"Yes, and that brings me to the second point about God's commandments, especially as you see them laid out in Jesus' sermon called the Sermon on the Mount. We can't obey them."

Alfred paused a moment.

"What do you mean we can't obey them?" Hank asked. "That's discouraging."

"Maybe," Alfred continued. "They will be discouraging until you finally get it."

"Get what," Hank asked.

"Trying to follow God's commandments can be very frustrating until you finally give up. When you realize you can't follow God's laws to the extent he expects, His law has done its duty. God's laws are designed for our well-being, but they can't be followed without him. God loves to fellowship with us and longs to live his life through us.

"In His economy, the universe is designed around Him. He desires to fellowship with us continually and only in this fellowship, only in our yielding to His Spirit within us, can we even begin to live the kind of life He desires for us to live."

There was a pause. Both stared ahead as the sky began to yield the pinks and light oranges of sunset.

"Tammy's been trying to tell me these things for a few years now," Hank said turning back and looking at his new friend. "But when she said it, it only made me mad. It makes no logical sense that God has set a standard for us we can never meet. Until recently, that just seemed cruel. When she said it, it repelled me and only made me close my heart up more to God and to her.

"But now it makes more sense. It actually endears me to her. I also wondered why, after how I treated our family, she still wanted us to be together. At least, until the last few months, when I guess the pain I caused her became too great.

"I just hope it's not too late. All I can think about is being with her and my kids."

"From what I know of Tammy so far," Alfred responded. "Your change of heart is exactly what she's been longing for."

Hank smiled.

"And what happened to Daniel was huge too!" Hank exclaimed. "Back to your original question about how I've changed. When he was missing and I was worried about his safety, I realized I had a love for him that had been crusted over and sent deep into my heart. In fact, I thought my love for him had died and certainly his love for me.

"It fed my feelings of failure and caused constant anger and arguments with him. However, I think we got a picture of how our relationship could be the other day when we visited Dr. Shuler's together. Again, I just hope it's not too late."

"I believe you can be at peace about what will happen with your family," Alfred said. "Ask God to guide your every step and wait, wait for his signal. If you're quiet and stay in tune, you'll see him around you and you'll hear him speak to your heart."

Hank nodded and they both turned their attention to the last remnants of orange sunlight rendering a sky line of shadows across the capital city.

After returning to Columbia, Peter spent the next couple of days helping Alice Jenkins prepare for Sarah's funeral, which was scheduled for Saturday in the upstate.

On Friday morning, Peter was in his office speaking with Mrs. Jenkins on the phone.

"Do you think Jacob Younginer will be there?" Alice asked.

"I don't know?" Peter answered. "I've tried calling his mom, but she hasn't returned my call.

"Have you had a chance to talk to your grandson about his mom?"

Alice was silent for a moment, as she fought back tears. When she finally spoke, all she could muster was a weak, "No. Not yet."

"Mrs. Jenkins, I'm leaving early tomorrow morning to get up there to help with the arrangements. And as you've asked, I've contacted the pastor about your wishes for the ceremony."

Alice didn't answer, but Peter could hear soft sobbing.

"I'll see you in the morning," Peter said. "Unfortunately, Elizabeth and the twins won't be able to come. They're heavily involved with a birthday party for one of their little friends. She's turning four."

"But when all this is over, you need to come spend a weekend with us. I can't wait for you to meet our twins."

Mrs. Jenkins could only muster a faint, "Okay."

"I should be there by 9:30. Call me if you need anything."

Peter hung up and returned to checking his e-mails. They had stacked up quite a bit since this whole adventure began with Cassie Eagan's call a week before.

So many things had happened in a week. Jimmy and Stephen Davis had resurrected the technology to send messages back in time. A technology he had so ardently tried to prevent because of the ramifications. His mysterious friend, Alfred, had reemerged with many words of encouragement. He met the Eagans and felt the pain of a family separated, yet forced to come together during the crisis of Daniel's kidnapping. He met Jacob Younginer and was exposed to his mysterious undelivered letters. He had a glimpse of the devastation of a couple who were desperately in-love, yet separated by a cruel twist of fate. And he experienced the devastating grief of the death of his lifelong friend, Sarah Jenkins.

Peter shook his head in disbelief. It had all happened so fast. It was the first time he'd paused to take an inventory of it all.

He decided to take a break and walk down to Alfred's condo, a few blocks from the university. He needed to clear his head and Alfred always had a way of helping him recalibrate his sight and his hopes.

Alfred had once told him that the secret of hope and joy is to have one and only one all-encompassing hope for your life, a hope that will not disappoint; a hope all lesser hopes can be built on. Alfred would often quote Romans 5:1-2:

"Therefore, since we have been justified by faith, we have peace with God through our Lord Jesus Christ. Through him we have also obtained access by faith into this grace in which we stand, and we rejoice in hope of the glory of God."

Alfred told him that since his wife Susan died, the hope of God's glory had become the hope of his life. He said that because of this choice, deep freedom and joy had been his companions, in spite of all circumstances.

Peter needed to hear this truth again from Alfred. Over the last few days, he'd seen a whole lot of hopes dashed.

As he turned the corner leading to the stairs descending to the ground floor of the Physics building, he heard, "Doc!"

It was Jimmy. Peter wanted to keep on going. He didn't need any more to sort through, but he stopped and turned back into the hallway and faced his colleague.

"Hey Jimmy, I thought you were off today."

"That's what I want people to think," smiled Jimmy.

"What do you mean?" Peter asked. A sinking feeling told him he already knew the answer to his question.

"We're ready," Jimmy smiled. "Calibrations are set, the satellite is in place and we'll be transmitting tonight."

"Jimmy!"

"Doc!" Jimmy cut him off with a smile. "I'm really not asking for your approval or your suggestions. Stephen and I have spent an inordinate amount of time weighing the possible ramifications of the event we plan on changing. We realize we can't predict how one changed event affects other events, but we're willing to take that risk. And we're not asking you to be involved in any way. However, we are telling you as a courtesy so that you'll be able to understand the fading memories you'll have of the event we're about to change."

"My memories? You mean the event affects me? Jimmy, please don't do this!"

It was no use. Jimmy had turned and was walking down the hall toward his office.

Meanwhile

"Hello." Tammy said as she picked up the phone.

"Tammy." Hank said as he stepped outside of his office building into the court yard.

"Hey Hank."

"How's Daniel?"

"He's doing okay. Every day he's more and more like himself."

"Has he hooked back up with his friends?"

"Yes, he had Mark over to play some video games this morning and they're still upstairs playing. I need to kick them outside soon."

"This whole adventure we've been on this last week seems to have had a positive effect on him," Hank replied. "He seems different. What do you think?"

"Absolutely!" Tammy agreed. "I think he was taking a whole lot for granted before last Friday."

"He's not the only one who was taking things for granted," Hank replied.

"Tammy," Hank said nervously, with an obvious change in tone.

"Yes, what is it Hank? You sound shaky."

"I am a bit shaky," Hank admitted. "I get this way sometimes with new beginnings."

"New beginnings?" she asked curiously.

"Yes. If you are not busy tonight, would you honor me with your presence for dinner at the Villa?"

Tammy paused long enough to send a sick pang to Hank's stomach, but then said. "I'd be delighted."

"I'll pick you up at 6:30. Will that work?"

"Perfect," Tammy replied.

TWENTY SEVEN

The next morning Peter woke up in a bit of a daze. He rolled over; expecting to see Elizabeth still asleep, but the bed was empty.

It was then he noticed the time and let out a yell of panic. It was 7:45. He should be leaving. Didn't he set the alarm for 6:00?

Suddenly, the bedroom door opened to a parade. Marching in first was Benjamin, carefully balancing a bowl of oatmeal on a small tray with a spoon on a folded cloth napkin. Instantly, the smell of coffee reached his nose and he saw Elizabeth with a mug filled with what had to be his favorite dark roast, already creamed. Little Sarah brought up the rear with the newspaper.

Peter smiled and did his best to acknowledge the gayety, but his thoughts were on his tardiness.

"What's this? What's the special occasion?"

"You," smiled Elizabeth, placing his coffee on the bedside table. "You're what's special. The twins and I agree that we couldn't ask for a better husband and father than you."

"We love you Daddy!" The twins screamed in unison.

Elizabeth took the tray from Benjamin and they both jumped on their father and gave him a patented 'Oreo hug', one on each side. "The good stuff's in the middle!" They screamed.

"I can't believe all this," Peter said after the laughter died down. "Guys, I love it, but I've over slept. I should've been on the road to Greenville fifteen minutes ago. I told Sarah's mom I'd be there by 9:30 to help with the last-minute arrangements."

"Relax, Peter," Elizabeth said. "Alice texted me a few minute ago. Everything is taken care of. If we leave by 9:00, we'll have plenty of time."

"We?" Peter questioned taking a sip of coffee. "I thought you and the twins were going to Timmy's birthday party."

Elizabeth came and sat down on the edge of the bed. By then the twins were scampering off the bed.

"You guys start getting dressed," she called to them as they disappeared around the corner of the hallway. "I'll be in to help you in a minute."

She then turned her attention to Peter. "You need to take a few more sips of coffee, Sweetie. You're still groggy. We talked about this last night. I've already talked to Timmy's mom and she certainly understands. This is an event we don't want to miss."

She leaned over and kissed him tenderly.

"If I can kiss you with your morning breath, topped off with dark coffee breath, you know I love you a whole lot."

Peter smiled.

"You relax a minute," She said. "Finish your breakfast. You seem a little out of it."

With that, Elizabeth left the room and shut the bedroom door.

Peter did feel out of it. He took another sip of coffee and a bite of oatmeal. When did he talk to Elizabeth about her and the twins coming to the funeral? He did remember something of the conversation, but the details escaped him. No matter now, he thought. Even if they weren't leaving for another hour or so, he needed to get going. He wanted to spend some more time thinking and praying about what he would say. Alice Jenkins had insisted he say a few words at Sarah's funeral.

Surprisingly enough to Peter, the family van pulled out of the driveway exactly when they were supposed to.

"This is a record. Have we ever really left when we said we would?" Peter asked as he shifted into drive after backing into the street.

"There're two things you should never be late to, your mother used to say," commented Elizabeth: "weddings and funerals."

"Yes, she did say that," Peter agreed, smiling slightly. He just wished it could have been the former and not the later.

A few minutes after Peter and his family turned onto I-26 East, Hank pulled out of the parking lot of his downtown condo, also heading to Greenville.

"Alfred, do me a favor," he said. "Look at that announcement in the side compartment of your door and tell me the name of the church again?"

"Buncombe Street Methodist," Alfred said, flipping the note over and looking at the other side. "Looks like we have plenty of time."

"Yes, I think we're in good shape. I just don't want to keep Cassie waiting. I told her we'd pick her up in a few minutes," Hank said.

"I'm sorry your wife and son aren't coming," Alfred said.

"Yes, I'm taking things real slowly," Hank said. "We had a great date last night at the Villa. It's our favorite restaurant. I took her there on our first date during our College years. I'm surprised the place is still there."

"It kind of felt like a first date last night," he continued. "I mean it had that first date excitement and newness. I felt like a teenager. But it was better than a first date, because we have history, much of it good."

"We ordered our favorite salads with black olives and chunks of yellow and white cheese. At the Villa we've always ordered a mixture of thousand island and blue cheese dressings."

"I was dreading a re-hashing of all I've done wrong, but not a word of it was mentioned. I felt like I was falling in love again."

Alfred smiled and even let out a laugh. "This is truly a miracle that things have turned around so quickly, especially compared to where you two were a week ago."

"I would have to agree," Hank smiled, switching on the radio.

When they arrived at the house to pick up Cassie, she came running to meet the car. Her smile arrived ahead of the rest of her.

Hank rolled down the driver side window.

"Mom wants to know if she can come too," Cassie asked. "She's already dressed.

"Of course she can!" Hank replied.

"We'll be out in a minute!" Cassie called out as she ran back toward the house.

Later in Greenville

Peter pulled into a parking place across a side street from the church. They were early and only a few cars were around. He got out and opened the door for Elizabeth. Then they each helped a twin get out of their back seat.

"Doc!"

Peter turned around and was surprised to see Jimmy and Stephen coming out of Jimmy's car a couple of spots over.

"I didn't know you guys were coming," Peter said. "That's very nice of you."

"We wouldn't miss this celebration," Jimmy smiled, seeming to look for a response from Peter.

"Honey, I'm going to go ahead and take the twins in," Elizabeth said. Ben has to go to the bathroom. "I'll meet you inside."

"Okay, Sweetie," he said, looking at his watch. "I won't be long."

Turning back to Jimmy and Stephen, he said, "Celebration?" He'd heard of a funeral being called a celebration of life, but he didn't think he would hear that kind of language from Jimmy.

"Doc, come over here and sit down. We have a few minutes. Stephen and I have something to talk to you about."

"Uh oh." Peter said, following them to a picnic table in the playground of the church. They sat down.

"Doc," Jimmy began. "Do you remember how confused we were when we changed time a few years ago?"

"Yes, I do. For a while we had two realities in our heads, the one that once was and the one that changed.

However, as time went on, the changed reality faded into our memories."

"What about the folks who didn't know about the transmission. Do you remember what happened to them?" Stephen asked.

"We never knew for sure, but we think the altered reality was more like a dream, subconscious thoughts with no index to pull them up, since they were unaware of the transmission.

"What are you getting at?" Peter asked nervously, looking at his watch. "I need to get inside. People are starting to arrive."

"Doc, what do you notice about the people who are starting to arrive?"

Peter looked around, but said nothing.

"Look at what they are wearing. Do they look like folks dressed for a funeral?"

"You changed something, didn't you?" Peter looked at them both. "You told me yesterday you were going to."

The events of the last few days were becoming increasingly more confused in Peter's mind.

"Yes, we did," Stephen said. "We did change a moment and we hope this change will be entirely good. But as you warned us, there's a risk other things may have changed, things we did not perceive."

"We took a risk, Doc," Jimmy said. "Already we know the change has created a whole new direction for life's events."

Peter tilted his head to the sky and began to moan, but Jimmy cut him short. "Come on, Doc," he said, lifting his senior colleague to his feet. "Let's go experience this together. The service is about to begin."

Before Peter could object, Stephen and Jimmy were ushering him toward the front door of the church. When they entered the narthex, Elizabeth and the twins were waiting on him.

Elizabeth smiled at Jimmy and Stephen, but didn't speak. The tone was quiet. They all took their place in line to enter the church.

On the other side of the church, Hank had parked his car and his crew was also walking toward the front door of the church, Hank and Tammy walking side by side with Alfred and Cassie following behind. As they turned the corner, along the serpentine walkway, Tammy reached over and grabbed Hank's hand.

Cassie looked over at Alfred and smiled.

Meanwhile, back at the Lexington County detention center, Bubba was once again being led to a questioning room to talk to an investigator.

This time, Detective Weed had some questions for him.

"Let's see here," Officer Weed said as he looked over Bubba's file and looked across the table at him. "Bobby, Bobby Manchester. But it says here they call you Bubba."

Bubba nodded.

"Mr. Manchester, can you tell me why you confessed to kidnapping Daniel Eagan."

Bubba tried to remain patient as he answered the same question again. "I was doing favors for MB in exchange for food and beer," he said. "And the favors went further than I expected."

"Why did you go further than you should have?" Detective Weed asked.

"I was afraid of him. He told me to get the letters back from the boy or else."

"Or else what?"

"He threatened me," Bubba answered. "He always carried a gun."

"And it says here these letters were letters you stole from a Postal Truck three years ago."

"Do you realize stealing mail is a felony?"

"That is what I was told," Bubba said.

"Do you know where Matt Baston could be hiding, the man you call MB?" Detective Weed asked.

A cold chill shivered his heart. Bubba thought he had heard MB was dead, but he couldn't recall exactly.

TWENTY EIGHT

"Daddy!" Benjamin shouted, a little too loudly, when he saw Peter enter the narthex with Jimmy and Stephen. Before Elizabeth could explain to him that he should keep his voice down, he and his twin sister had already darted over and were hugging their daddy's knees.

Stephen, standing next to Jimmy, as they all filed toward the signing register, was deep in thought. He and Jimmy had flawlessly made the transmission last night at the exact planned time: 11:23 PM. The message, sent back in the form of pulses of Morse code light in the skies of May 17th, 1982, were meant to save Sarah's life.

Searching his memory of last weekend on Kiawah Island, when he and Peter had encountered a speeding Matt Baston with Sarah in the car, he could gain no clarity. Had he successfully interfered with the chase as his message to himself had instructed? Or had they failed. His memory contained scrambled pieces of both outcomes. But what was real, what was reversed, what was planned?

He remembered Peter and him being surprised by the speeding Matt Baston with Sarah in the car whizzing by them, followed by the lights and siren of the deputy's car. That was the outcome that led to Sarah and Matt Baston's death when the car was rammed a few minutes later.

But he also remembered another outcome. An outcome in which he'd parked his car sideways across the road before Matt Baston's car arrived. In that outcome, he and Peter had gotten out of the parked car, watching from the side of the road as Matt Baston's Lexus screeched to a stop to avoid hitting it. Trees on either side of the road blocked his escape and all he could do was dart from the car on foot and sprint into the wooded area toward the western end of the island.

But was that outcome real?

"Come on."

Stephen was suddenly aware of Jimmy motioning to him to get in line to enter the church.

"I signed your name too," Jimmy said, laying down the pen on the sign in register "What were you doing, daydreaming?"

"I guess so," Stephen responded. "I'm trying to make sense of all the conflicting memories in my head."

"It must be worse for the person who receives the message from the future," Jimmy noted. "And I can see why. You've had a new reality ever since you saw our message from last night, even if it was just a message for you to do something to change an outcome. It was new information you've carried around in your head for over 30 years."

Stephen nodded and Jimmy continued. "For me, the change is recent. I understand it clearly."

By then Peter and his family had entered the church.

A young man dressed in a blue tuxedo trimmed in white reached out for Elizabeth to take his arm.

"This is no funeral!" Peter said under his breathe, a flood of confused excitement literally knocked his head.

"Bride or grooms side?" the young man asked Elizabeth.

"Bride side," Elizabeth responded with a smile, looking back at Peter.

Peter was absolutely stunned. As he and the twins followed Elizabeth and the groomsman to their seat, Peter looked around at all the yellow roses, beautifully lining the outer aisles. Sarah's favorite.

This wasn't Sarah's funeral. This was her wedding.

A middle-aged woman stood up in the corner, to the right of Peter and his family as they sat down. She positioned a viola and the sound of "Jesu, Joy of Man's Desiring" softly and smoothly filled the church.

Peter felt a hand grab his right shoulder, give a firm squeeze and a slight shake. He looked up and saw Alfred smiling at him. They exchanged a look of amazement. Alfred holding Cassie's hand, caught up with Hank as they followed Tammy in a groomsman's arm.

As they passed, Peter caught a glimpse of Cassie. He wasn't sure if he could remember a bigger smile on anyone's face his entire life. She was double delighted.

Delighted that her parents were together with her and delighted for this wedding event she'd hoped for and so vehemently fought for.

Hank waited for Tammy to enter the aisle on the groom's side and he followed closely behind her. Cassie let loose of Alfred's hand and followed her parents to the middle of the row.

"Can you believe how quickly this wedding came together?" Elizabeth whispered to Peter. "Look at the details. Alice said it took a bit of work to find tuxedo's that shade of blue. The bride's maid dresses are the color of the roses; blue and yellow, Sarah's favorite colors."

Sarah. She's okay. Peter thought. How did Stephen and Jimmy do it? It's got to be Jacob she's marrying. But he was in such bad shape the last time he saw him. Hopeless they had called him, but events had changed from then.

Jimmy and Stephen were now walking down the center aisle to sit down. Jimmy was intently scanning the crowd, looking left, but focusing more as he looked right.

"Here," he said to Stephen, pointing to an aisle a couple of rows back from where Alfred and the Eagans were now seated. They slid into the end of the aisle.

"There," Jimmy whispered to Stephen as they sat down, nodding his head toward a man seated at the end of the row ahead of them.

Stephen looked at the man, clad in a wide-brimmed black hat looking straight ahead. He wondered what Jimmy meant, but didn't respond.

Peter felt a tap on his shoulder and looked up to see Alice Jenkins standing over him.

"Peter, can you come with me," she said with a smile.

Peter stood up and looked down at Elizabeth. She only nodded and also smiled. Did she know something he didn't?

Peter followed Alice to the narthex. Already the three groomsmen were assembled next to their assigned bride's maids. Each maid was brightly arrayed in canary yellow dresses. Peter followed Alice through a door at the side of the narthex.

Back in the sanctuary, Tammy reached over and took Hank's hand. He felt like a school boy who learns the girl he couldn't keep his eyes off of, likes him. After so many years of marriage, how could he feel this way? Where was the newness coming from?

The music changed and out of a door ahead of Hank and to his right, emerged a clergyman, dressed in a white robe trimmed in red, followed by Jacob and his best man. Still not a hundred percent, Jacob's head was bandaged and he walked tentatively. His best man, a tall well-built man, followed him closely.

The procession of groomsmen and bride's maids began. As each groomsman passed in front of Jacob he met their glances with a knowing acknowledgment of their dedicated friendship. Jacob's knees began to shake a bit as he strained to hold his emotions in. His best man steadied him with a supportive arm behind, ready to hold him up if needed.

As the wedding party took their places, yellow gowns to the left and blue tuxedos to the right, a hush filled the sanctuary. As a new song proceeded softly from the organ, a little boy of about three years emerged, facing Jacob at the back of the church. He too was adorned in the smallest of blue tuxedos, an exact match in color and style to the groomsmen. In his little hands was a yellow pillow with a blue ribbon holding down a ring.

Jacob's lips began to quiver and the arm around him stiffened. The little boy began to slowly amble to the front. His grandmother, now seated as the mother of the bride, stood up and urged him on. When he saw her, the boy's face brightened. When he made it to the front, Alice scooped him up and positioned him near his dad with the groomsmen.

At Alice's right, Betty Younginer wiped a tear, but tried to hold it all in for her son's sake.

All heads then turned when "The Bridal March" began. Following Alice Jenkin's lead, the congregation rose to their feet. A gasp came over the crowd at the sight they beheld. Sarah, arrayed in a snow-white wedding dress with yellow shoes, stood in stunning beauty before them. Her golden hair was pulled back and she held a bouquet of yellow roses, trimmed with white lace. Her left arm was wrapped around Peter's right arm and he held her glove laced hand.

As they moved slowly toward the front of the church, the arm around Jacob stiffened and he was held upright. Jacob could see his bride through his watered eyes and to him she was moving in slow motion. He was fighting a memory that she had died and that this long-awaited moment wouldn't and couldn't be happening. But it was happening. He'd dreamed of it thousands of times. Though hope had waned, almost extinguished, it had never died.

As Peter and Sarah approached the front, the man in the black hat seated in front of Jimmy, slid his hand slowly inside the breast pocket of his jacket and felt the gun. He grabbed the handle and slipped his index finger around the trigger, but did not pull it out. Not yet.

As Peter and Sarah stood before him, the minister said, "Welcome friends of Sarah Jenkins and Jacob Younginer Hope."

Jacob looked down at his mother with a smile of acknowledgment. It was the first time he'd heard his true name. He was happy he'd taken the time to have it officially changed in spite of the busyness of the week.

The name Hope took the man in the black hat by surprise. He squeezed hard around the handle and slowly pulled the gun out of his coat pocket. As he did, his left hand covered it from sight.

TWENTY NINE

"Sarah and Jacob want to welcome you to this joyous occasion," the minister continued. "And they want to thank you for being here in spite of the late notice."

The man in the black hat readied the pistol resting on his stomach, hidden by his left hand.

"We've done some research," the minister continued. "We think this is a record for the most glamorous wedding put together in a week."

The minister looked over at Jacob and asked, "So you asked her to marry you a week ago, when you were in the hospital in Charleston?"

"Actually, I asked her three years ago," Jacob replied, "But she just didn't answer me until last Saturday."

"Wow, it took you that long to ponder the question?" the minister joked, looking at Sarah.

"Not exactly," Sarah smiled."

"We'll I'm sure the longing and waiting has made this time even sweeter. You may all sit down." He motioned to the crowd with his hands.

This is what the man in the black hat, Matt Baston, was waiting on. His index finger was on the trigger, but it seemed the crowd took forever to sit down. When they finally did, he raised his hand and took aim, but the shot was not clear. Up ahead, directly in between him and Jacob, a black man remained standing, facing the bride and groom. Quickly Matt moved to his right, standing up slightly, seeking a clear shot.

As he raised his arm again to aim, it was suddenly brought down with such force, that the gun was knocked out of his hand, hitting the pew and falling innocently to the carpet next to a stained-glass window on the outer aisle. Jimmy quickly grabbed Matt Baston in a tight bear hug. Witnesses would later recount that they heard something crack, perhaps a rib. At any rate, Matt Baston couldn't move.

There were sudden screams and crowd movements, but the disruption was over almost as soon as it had begun. Taking Peter's advice, Jimmy had thought through every angle of what would change if he and Stephen saved Sarah's life. And the most glaring change was the fact that if the crash didn't happen, Matt Baston would also be spared. Not understanding Baston's motives, but knowing his evil intentions toward Sarah and Jacob, he felt their wedding would be a prime event for him to strike.

In fact, his whole reason for being at the wedding was for protection. He'd contacted the police of the city of Greenville and convinced them to be on standby.

As he held the struggling Matt Baston, two plain clothed policeman, who had been observing the ceremony from the back of the church, rushed in and quickly took over. They pulled Baston into the aisle and led him, struggling, out of the sanctuary.

After the noise died down, it became apparent that Sarah was very visibly shaken. She was seated; head down, on one of the steps leading to the altar with Jacob, her mother and Peter trying to comfort her. Jacob was more than a little rattled, seeing the man who had put him in the hospital only a few days before pointing a gun in his general direction. But seeing Sarah crumbling in Peter's arms, he forgot about himself and rushed to attend to her.

Water was brought in to refresh her and she was allowed to rest until she was ready.

When Sarah gained her strength, and took her place again beside Peter, the minister waved his hand for silence. "That was unexpected," he said. "But, with these two and what they've been through, it seems a bit normal.

He smiled warmly, looking first at Sarah and then at Jacob.

"Who gives this woman to this man?"

"I do," Alice Jenkins said standing and locking eyes with Sarah.

Peter handed Sarah's hand to Jacob and returned to his seat with Elizabeth and the twins.

"Sarah and Jacob," the minister began. "I don't know the full story, but I know enough to know your love for each other has weathered some significant storms."

"You had a disagreement a few years ago that shattered your relationship, seemingly forever. By a twist of fate, which I still don't really understand, each of you was led to believe the other's love had grown cold.

"In the years you were apart, you tried to move on. However, rather than fade, your love grew. With the discovery of Jacob's lost letter, a little over a week ago, events were set in motion that would bring you back together."

"Though," the minister turned and looked at Jacob, "these events were painful and dangerous. I have been told by both of you individually that you would have endured much more than what you've been through to have this opportunity to proclaim your undying love before God and these witnesses."

The minister went on to give a brief charge to the couple and lead them through their vows. He wisely kept the service shorter than he usual because he could tell Jacob was growing weary.

When at last Sarah and Jacob kissed, her in a flowing white gown, laced in yellow and he in his blue tuxedo, separated from the rest of the guys by his yellow rose boutonnière, the moment was magical. Every couple in the audience squeezed the hand of their sweetheart, no matter how many years they'd been together, especially Hank and Tammy.

The kiss was delicate, but penetrating. It had a mesmerizing effect. No one could quite recall how long it lasted.

"And now, may I present to you Mr. and Mrs. Jacob Hope and their son Bryan."

Sarah held out her arms and scooped up little Bryan in a tender embrace, then let him down beside her. She grabbed his hand and slipped her other arm in her husband's and they marched out.

The crowd let loose resounding applause and began to file out for the reception in the adjoining fellowship hall.

Along the way Alfred caught up with Peter and his family.

"Alfred!" Peter said, as he noticed him. "Finally, I get to introduce two amazingly important people in my life to each other. Honey, this is Alfred. Alfred, this is my lovely wife, Elizabeth."

Alfred approached Elizabeth to shake her hand, but she would have none of that. With a beaming smile, she moved past his outstretched hand and gave him a huge hug.

"Alfred. I have been so looking forward to meeting you, though I must admit for a while I thought Peter was making you up."

"Why is that?" Alfred asked as they continued their way down the hall to the reception.

"You've made such an impact on Peter's life, especially a few years ago, that I keep asking Peter if I could meet you. But Peter couldn't make it happen."

"But you know I tried," Peter added with a laugh, walking behind them with a twin on either hand. "I was starting to wonder myself if I'd made you up in my mind. I'm glad in more ways than one that you showed up a week or so ago."

"I've been out of communication the last few years," Alfred admitted. "I'm sure Peter told you I was in Atlanta?"

"Yes, and I'm so sorry to hear of your wife's death. Are you doing okay?"

"I miss her every day," Alfred admitted.

"Hello," Benjamin broke free of his daddy's hand and was now pulling at Alfred's pant leg.

"Hello," little Sarah copied her twin and was tugging on his other leg.

"Hello!" Alfred smiled, picking up one and then the other.

"Sorry Alfred," Peter said. "They were actually being very patient. They love people and I should've introduced you to them. They've actually been talking about meeting you as much as Elizabeth. What were you saying about Susan?"

"No problem," Alfred said, now delighting in swinging the twins around in his arms. "I was just going to say that reconnecting with you and meeting the Eagans has made my grief so much easier."

"Eagans?" Elizabeth asked.

"They're the ones who found Jacob's letter," Peter replied.

"Oh yes. I'd like to meet them too," she replied. "This has been quite an adventurous week for you all. You picked a great time to show back up, Alfred."

"I knew I needed to be here," he said with a smile, setting the twins down as they entered the reception hall.

"Can Mr. Alfred stay with us awhile, Mommy?" Sarah asked.

Elizabeth looked at Alfred and said. "Mr. Alfred can stay with us whenever he wants for as long as he wants."

After the wedding party was introduced, guests lined up to greet the new family.

Near the front of the line Cassie waited patiently, her parents on either side; Hank finishing up a few meat balls left on his plate, Tammy nursing a glass of lemonade punch.

"Hey!" Cassie said, looking right at Jacob and then glancing at Sarah when she made it to the front of the line.

"Hey Cassie," Jacob said with excitement.

"How're you feeling?" Cassie asked.

"I'm feeling better every moment I'm with this beautiful lady," Jacob said, pulling Sarah close.

"Cassie!" Sarah exclaimed. "It is so great to meet you. Jacob has told me all about you. You're like our hero. It was you who would not give up on making sure I read Jacob's letter. Thank you!"

Cassie blushed a bit, but answered. "I could really tell from the letter how much Jacob loves you. And somehow I just knew you loved him too. So, I couldn't give up trying to make sure you read it."

"Yes, she was quite determined," spoke up Hank from behind Cassie. "Excuse me for butting in, but I'm Cassie's father, Hank, and this is her mother, Tammy."

"Pleased to meet you both," Sarah said. "Truly, I'm pretty sure we wouldn't be standing here right now if it wasn't for your Cassie. I'm very thankful she didn't give up."

"She's a very determined young lady," Tammy said. "We all love her for it. She never seems to give up hope."

THIRTY

Approximately six months later - Kiawah Island

"Sarah and I are extremely excited you could all come," Jacob said as the wine was poured and he readied his toast. "For a while now we've wanted to have you down to Sarah's mom's condo to thank each of you for your part in our reunion and subsequent wedding.

"Stephen and Jean, thank you for opening up your condo as well. This allows us all to be lodged quite comfortably. And though we love our children, we are also happy that with various combinations of grandparents and sitters, we can enjoy a weekend as couples only."

Jacob stood up with his wine glass raised and looked around the table. To his right, his bride Sarah smiled and looked up proudly at her husband. Seated next to Sarah sat Peter flanked by his bride, Elizabeth. Then there was Jimmy's wife, Marlee. Seated next to Marlee and across the table from Jacob, sat Jimmy. Next to Jimmy sat Stephen, along with his wife, Jean. And finally, seated at Jacob's left were the Eagans. Tammy and Hank, just back from their second honeymoon.

"First, I would like to toast my lovely bride on this grand occasion of our first half anniversary," Jacob raised his glass of burgundy and lightly connecting his glass with

Sarah, Hank and then as many others as he could reach across the table.

The others followed his example and everyone took a sip.

"Next, I'd like to toast you, our guests, for your roles in our magical reunion. Peter Anderson, I toast you for being the connecting point that helped the Eagans find Sarah and for your continual help and support throughout the whole eventful weekend."

As before, Jacob led the group in clinking glasses and all enjoyed the expensive wine Jacob had secured for the occasion.

"Next, I would like to thank Jimmy Bouillion, who most probably saved my life at our wedding. He was alert enough to strong arm Matt Baston before he could shoot me."

Jacob tipped his glass again toward Sarah and then toward Jimmy. All then repeated the toasting, done twice before. New wine was poured in a few glasses by the culinary staff Jacob had employed from the Sanctuary Inn located in the middle of the Island.

Looking at Jimmy, Jacob said, "The unusual thing about it is that neither Sarah nor I actually remember inviting you to our wedding."

"However, we're certainly glad you decided to crash it."

Everyone laughed.

"What I'd like to know," Jimmy said after his swallow of wine, "Is why Alfred didn't sit down when everyone else did. He was standing directly in the line of fire between Matt Baston's gun and you. If he hadn't been there, I think Baston would have gotten the shot off before I could stop him.

"Doc, did you get a chance to ask him, why he didn't sit down?"

"No, I sure didn't," Peter replied. "But Alfred has an uncanny way of knowing when people need help."

"He sure does," agreed Hank. "He helped me understand how selfish and prideful I was being. Without him, I'm not sure Tammy and I would be back together. I was in a bad way.

"Why couldn't he join us?"

"He was tied up helping a fellow he met downtown at the mission," Jacob replied. "He would definitely be getting a toast if he were here."

"This brings me to another wedding crasher," Jacob said, again raising his glass. "Stephen Davis. To be honest, I'm not really sure what Stephen did to contribute to our reconciliation and wedding. But, he and his wife Jean are marvelous people, who live here at Kiawah Island full time. Peter tells me that you definitely had a role and that I should trust him on that. So, trust him I do. Here, here."

Again there was clinking and sipping all around.

"And finally, so that we can stop our toasting and begin eating, I come to the Eagan's, Cassie, Daniel, Tammy and Hank." Jacob raised his glass. "This whole adventure has been such a wondrously difficult and exciting one, especially for Sarah and me. But truly it would not have happened if two children playing in the woods behind their house hadn't seen my lost letter in the gleam of the setting sun. Against all odds, my message found its way to Sarah's heart. And to my great astonishment, a spark remained of a dying love. With the help of you all, but especially the Eagan's, two broken hearts were mended. And our love, now restored, is far stronger than ever."

Jacob raised his glass, signaling the final toast.

When all had toasted the Eagan family, the first course was served. The room was filled with the aroma of fresh baked French bread. The bread was accompanied with plenty of soft butter and a salad of spinach, pralines and strawberries.

Jacob asked Peter to give thanks for the food. Hands were joined around the table. Peter thanked the Lord for His great love, for the miraculous reunion of Sarah and Jacob, for the new friendships and finally for the food.

When eating was well underway, Jacob interrupted the conversations and said, "In addition to gathering you all to show our gratitude for your part in our wedding and to celebrate our first 6 months, there is something else I would like to accomplish."

Everyone stopped talking, even staying their utensils as they listened.

"Please keep eating. This is something we can discuss as we continue to enjoy this delicious food."

"As you know, just before Sarah and I got married, I discovered that I'm adopted. I'm actually a Hope. With some help from Hank's lawyer friend, I was even able to officially change my name to Hope before the wedding. Sarah and I think we have some answers as to how Matt Baston got involved in our story. And we want to tell you about it. We also want to hear from Jimmy, who recently visited Baston in jail."

"Also, Hank and Daniel recently visited Dr. Shuler's mother, my great Aunt Polly, and he has a bit of Hope family lore he would like to tell us."

Jacob took a bite of his salad and reached for a slice of bread, then continued.

"Hank, would you mind telling us what you found out?"

"Not at all," Hank replied. "Let me start out by saying that over the last few months, Daniel and I, and sometimes Cassie, have spent a lot of time with your aunt. She is a delightful southern lady who has been through much in her life. I believe what I'm about to relay to you is a story she would have been very content to have left unsaid and carry to her grave. However, she and Daniel have become very close. Daniel loves her stories and she is quite impressed with the young man he's become."

Hank smiled at Tammy and said, "This is a recent development in Daniel's character which we are quite proud of."

"I'm proud of you," Tammy said. "Since you started showing such love to Daniel, he's become a different person."

"I'm afraid I can't take credit for that," Hank said sincerely. "But I'm most thankful."

"Anyway, back to what Aunt Polly told us."

Hank looked at Jacob, took a bite of salad and continued.

"Lore has it that in the eighteenth century a large Swedish family migrated to the Broad River basin, along Hollenshed Creek in the area we call now Dutch Fork. This family, the Hopes, traveled south from Pennsylvania seeking warmer temperatures. Among the Hope clan was the John Hope family with his wife Deborah. Of all the Hopes who migrated south, they experienced the most hardship. Originally Deborah and John had three sons and two daughters. However, through illnesses, an Indian attack and the death of a daughter during child birth, they were left with one remaining child, their youngest son Charles. John and Deborah were devastated. John fought temptations to give up. It took all he could muster to maintain the courage needed to provide for his family. Some days he was so disheartened he couldn't get out of bed. The rest of the Hope clan did what they could to help Deborah and Charles with the chores. John's brothers and Uncles would drop off food as they could from their hunting trips. The John Hope family was in a bad way and their home site was growing more and more dilapidated."

Hank took a sip of wine and Tammy looked at him admiringly.

"Among the settlers already in the Dutch Fork area when the Hope family arrived were Germans who had migrated south, mostly because of the free fifty acre incentives offered to populate what was then considered the back country."

"You sound like an announcer from the history channel," joked Peter.

"Hank loves history and he's been doing a lot of research from what Aunt Polly told him," Tammy said.

"History is fascinating," said Hank "Especially when you can link it to real people.

"I found out that 'Deutsch' means 'German' and it is pronounced Dutch. And 'Fork' referred to the land lying between the Broad and Saluda rivers. That's how Dutch Fork got its name."

"Very cool," replied Marlee. "I love stuff like this. Please go on."

"Very well," smiled Hank. "Among the German families already settled when the Hopes arrived was a weaver named Jerg Hipp. Jerg and his wife Anna had five sons and one daughter named Angel. Angel was gifted with unusual beauty and her brothers were quite protective of her.

"In general, the Germans who lived in the area weren't fond of outside settlers. So, when the Hope clan arrived, there was much resentment among the locals. Their dreams of establishing an exclusively German population was being thwarted and they weren't happy. In fact, they were angry.

"Jerg Hipp was the leader of a smaller subset of the German population who established a secret society to eradicate all non-Germans from the Dutch Fork area, especially the Hopes who had 'invaded' in such numbers. And as fate would have it, the John Hope family was Jerg Hipp's closest neighbor, having their tract of land just across the Hollenshed creek. The continual dilapidation of the John Hope cabin, which could be seen through the clearing from the Hipp side of the creek, didn't help Jerg's resentment.

"As legend has it, Angel Hipp was swimming in the creek on a June morning in 1749 when Charles came upon her as he led his horse down to the creek for a drink. Charles was instantly captivated by her beauty and silently watched her while she continued to swim, unaware of his presence."

Hank paused a moment to finish off his piece of buttered bread, then continued.

Jacob, taking the pause as an opportunity, said. "Hank, excuse me just a moment. I hate to interrupt you, but I've just been informed that our main course is ready. Let's take a short commercial break."

This was followed by some sarcastic boos from the group, who'd become enthralled in Hank's tale.

Jacob laughed. "That's the first time I'm sure that these servers have had objections to their main course being served, but under the circumstances, I completely understand. If Hank ever grows tired of being a computer programmer, I'm sure he could get a job as a historian and story teller."

For the next little while there was laughter, glasses of water poured and the main course served. It consisted of filet mignon, fresh off the grill, cooked to order. The steak was flanked by mashed red potatoes with the skin still on, followed by asparagus with hollandaise sauce.

As soon as the plates were laid out, Hank was asked to continue.

"Let him take a few bites," Sarah replied, always looking for ways to be considerate.

"It's okay Sarah," Hank replied, before he took his first bite of steak. I can eat and talk."

"Just don't do it at the same time," chided Tammy jokingly.

"Of course not," Hank replied, his mouth still full of steak as he spoke.

Everyone chuckled.

Hank finished off his broccoli and took a few more bites of his steak before he continued.

"After a while, Angel became aware of Charles staring at her. She was startled, but not afraid. Angel didn't share her families' disdain for non-German settlers. In fact, she'd met Charles' mother, Deborah Hope, in town. The closest town was located in an area between present day Irmo and Lexington, now covered by Lake Murray. Angel and Deborah had become friends and they'd often talk, as long as Angel's family wasn't around.

"Angel had learned of John Hope's deep depression. Deborah told her about their only remaining child, Charles. And she assumed it was he who was watching her from Deborah's description.

"She said hello. He returned the greeting and they had a casual conversation across the creek that day. When Charles returned home, he told his mother about meeting Angel. He told of her captivating beauty and how he couldn't get her out of his mind. His mother was delighted. She liked Angel and considered her heart far more beautiful than her stunning outward appearance."

"Sarah," Peter interrupted. "That was one of the first things Jacob said to me about you."

Sarah turned to Jacob and kissed him. The dinner party responded with a unified "Awwwww….."

Hank took advantage of the lull to take a bite of his potatoes and another couple of bites of steak. When he looked up, all eyes were on him to continue.

"Charles and Angel ran in to each other several other times, mainly because they had both figured when they might spot the other. Their conversations became longer and longer and both were growing more and more drawn to each other.

"Still in secret, Charles and Angel began to plan meetings, spending afternoons along the creek, telling stories and sharing feelings. Then one August afternoon, they planned a ride together along the shores of the Broad River toward what is now downtown Columbia."

"Unfortunately, Jerg Hipp had now become suspicious of Angel's comings and goings. That afternoon, he ordered one of his sons, Jonas, to follow Angel to see what she was up to.

"Jonas followed Angel long enough to see her ride off with Charles and reported it back to his father. Jerg was livid. Not only had these Hopes invaded the area, but the son of the laziest of them, John Hope, had ridden off with his daughter."

"Jerg called together his group of militant Germans and together they made plans to rid themselves of all the Hopes. Not only had they invaded 'Deutsch' Fork, but now there were threats of interbreeding. This would mean the further spoiling of their native race.

"They determined to begin their scare tactics as soon as Angel returned. Murder was not the plan, at least at first. Starting with the John Hope family, they were to burn all buildings, except the main dwellings: outhouses, barns, chicken coops and the like. The clear message was to be 'get out of here or else'.

"Hipp's men would be sent out in twos with torches to every Hope home site, ready to burn when the signal came. There were some in the group who wondered why the main dwellings needed to be spared. This would send a stronger message, they urged. And so the seeds of destruction were sown."

Hank finished off his steak and took another bite of his potatoes before he continued. "In the meantime, Angel's horse, who had historically suffered from bone spavins, slowed down to a walk an hour or so into the ride. Charles and Angel waited for some time, hoping the horse would recover. However, as the sun began to set, they began a slow trek home.

"When Angel was not at home by dark, Jerg's anger turned to pure rage. Thinking Angel had run off with the Hope boy, Jerg set the plan in motion. News of Angel's disappearance spread like wild fire among the conspirators, morphing as it went. As the news circulated, Angel went from being kidnapped to being murdered and a savage tipping point was reached.

"Starting with the John Hope home site, every Hope building in the Dutch Fork area was torched, including the main dwellings. The evil escalated like wolves – crazy over flowing blood. Hopes were being shot as they fled their burning tombs.

"The sight of smoke in the moonless night was hidden from Charles and Angel as they slowly rode. However, as they neared home they saw the light from the burning buildings and an acrid smell filled their noses. They quickened their pace and as they neared the spot they often met, they heard a female voice on the Hipp side of the creek. It was Anna Hipp, Angel's mother. She came to warn them. She told them what had happened and that Charles' parents were both dead. She also said she heard some of the ruffians threatening to kill Angel if she wasn't already dead. She urged them to flee.

"Anna Hipp quickly gave them some food and they left on Charles' horse. Days later, when they reached the upstate, they were married.

"Anna Hipp organized a group of people to bury the murdered Hopes. They dug graves on either side of Hollenshed Creek, not far from the John Hope home site.

"Aunt Polly knows that Charles and Angel Hope survived. But the assault against the Hopes didn't end that night. It has continued over the years. From unexplained deaths to downright murder, Hopes haven't been safe in this area."

"Does she think descendants from the Hipp family have kept the killing going?" Stephen asked.

"She doesn't know," Hank replied, taking a last bite of potatoes and finishing his wine. "But with the letter Jacob found in his grandfather's attic, we know other families have championed the evil cause. Aunt Polly knew enough to know that the Younginers were a threat. She believed the Hopes weren't safe. Jacob, you were the sole surviving male Hope. That's why Aunt Polly was an integral part of arranging your adoption, even into a family she suspected. By concealing your identity, she thought being loved by the Younginers would keep you safe."

Hank took the last few bites of his meal. The others remained silent, taking in the story which had unfolded.

After a while, Jacob motioned to the servers. "That fills in much of the beginning of the story. Let's have some desert and coffee. After we're served we'll try and piece together the more recent parts."

THIRTY ONE

"What is the name of this coffee?" Marlee asked the server. "It's so dark and rich."

"I wish I could tell you, ma'am," he replied. "It's a special blend served only at the Sanctuary. Our owners have an exclusive agreement with a coffee plantation in Brazil."

"Isn't it amazing," Jean Davis replied. "Stephen and I sometimes walk down to the inn just for the coffee. We can't get it anywhere else."

"Wonder what the difference is?" Marlee asked. "The flavor is so deep, yet not the hint of bitterness."

"I overheard a couple of the waiters say it has to do with the timing of both the picking and the roasting of the beans, but that's about all I know," said Stephen.

Marlee looked across the table hoping to catch the server's eye for confirmation, but without success.

After the coffee, chocolate mousse topped with black cherry liqueur compote and freshly whipped cream was served.

Following the elegance and etiquette of a true southern meal, all spoons were stayed until Sarah took the first bite. Jimmy, a country boy from Louisiana, became painfully aware of the proper order via Marlee's elbow in his side.

After a couple of bites, followed by praise of the dessert and murmurs of decadence, Jacob interrupted the conversations. "Now, let me tell you what I know about Matt Baston and how he got involved.

"Matt Baston wasn't initially obsessed with the Hope family lore. Baston had an obsession all right, but it wasn't with the Hope family, it was with Sarah."

As if on cue, Jacob looked over at Sarah and she continued the story. "I met Matt when I was in a mental hospital after suffering a nervous breakdown. As Peter can tell you, I experienced some tragic family circumstances which I couldn't handle. My mind literally had a meltdown, like a heart attack; only it involved my brain. I was out of it for a long time.

"Matt suffers from a bipolar condition which produces acute psychosis if not controlled by medication. In the hospital, he believed he was a James Bond type figure. And I was strangely attracted to him. We spent a lot of time together and even talked of getting together after we were released from the hospital.

"The doctors were able to figure out the right combinations of medicine for Matt and he began to even out mentally. He became more rational and I remained attracted to him.

"He was released before I was and we made our plans to meet up once I got out. However, my time at the mental hospital didn't end in the traditional way, which is a story for another time."

Sarah smiled at Peter, who knew what she was referring to. She then took another bite of mousse and continued.

"Let's just say I ended up in New York and lost touch with Matt."

Sarah took another sip of coffee and a server filled her cup.

"Eventually, I moved back to South Carolina and tried to find Matt. One evening, I saw him at Five Points with another woman.

"This was very hard to handle, but after much soul searching, I decided to move on with my life. Soon after that, I met Jacob and fell hopelessly in love."

"Tag," Sarah said, looking over at Jacob with a smile.

"Consider us like tag team wrestlers in this story," Jacob chuckled. "Sarah just tagged me, so I'm to continue; mostly because Sarah wants to finish her dessert."

This drew a few chuckles as Sarah nodded in agreement and polished off a bite.

"As you all know, Sarah and I planned to marry over three years ago, but I wasn't ready. What I didn't know then was that Sarah was pregnant.

"When she found out, she began to talk more seriously about marriage. But I, being a selfish bachelor, wasn't ready for commitment. I knew she was the one I wanted to spend the rest of my life with, but I needed more time.

"However, with Bryan growing inside of her, Sarah didn't have time. When I told her I wasn't ready for marriage, Sarah was devastated. In her pain, she chose to break away from me. And who could blame her?"

"To add to her pain, a coworker of mine, named Cindy plotted to take advantage of the situation. She showed up at my place uninvited. I wasn't sure at first what she was up to. Looking back, I never should have even opened the door. But I did and then I couldn't get her to leave. Then Sarah showed up unexpectedly."

"She saw Cindy and you can imagine what that did to her. In her mind, she had been quickly pushed aside. She moved back to Columbia and wouldn't answer any of my calls. Within days, I realized I couldn't live without her. Since she wouldn't answer my calls, I got her new address from her mother and decided to write her a letter asking for her forgiveness and formally asking her to marry me."

"It was that letter that Cassie and Daniel found undelivered in the abandoned cabin in the woods behind their house."

"And, as fate would have it, this was the same week I discovered my great Uncle Luke's letter in my grandfather's attic. It was the first I heard of the Hope family legend. It was intriguing. I did a little research and discovered that the grave sites referred to in Uncle Luke's document really did exist and had been discovered in 1919. The cause of all the deaths of one family was considered an unsolved mystery. But I held in my hand a clue which might solve it. I couldn't find anyone named Hope in the midlands area of South Carolina who could have been descendants of those massacred. But I did discover that Dr. Shuler's mother was a Hope."

"Aunt Polly," interjected Hank.

Jacob nodded. "But then the break up with Sarah occurred and I didn't have the heart for anything. In fact, I'm surprised I didn't lose my job. I was a shell of a man. I had no energy or motivation to deal with life's daily duties, much less solving a long-lost murder mystery.

"So I wrote the letter to Dr. Shuler the same day I wrote my letter to Sarah and dropped them together in the mail. But little did I know .... Tag."

Sarah, now finished with her dessert, picked up the story. "I'm going to pick back up on my encounter with Matt. When I saw him with that other woman at Five Points, I didn't realize he had seen me too. He had me tracked. Matt employed pitiful, addicted men to do his bidding. His family is filthy rich and he's always been able to pay for whatever he wants."

"He tracked me to Charleston and discovered Jacob had become my boyfriend. And from that moment on, Jacob became his number one enemy. Phil, one of Matt's minions, worked at the Charleston Post office. He was instructed to monitor Jacob's mail, looking for anything that would discredit or destroy him."

"In his mind," Jacob picked up the story, "I was the devil himself. So you can imagine what happened when his 'spy' informed him of my letter to Sarah. He wasn't even interested in my letter to Dr. Shuler, at least at the time. Both letters were carefully opened, photocopied and resealed."

"When Matt was informed of the contents of both letters, he had even more reason to shut me down. Not only had I stolen his girl, but now he thought my family was involved in an egregious plot. It brought justification to his hatred for me.

"Why didn't Phil just keep the letters and not put them back into circulation?" asked Elizabeth; "seems like that would have been easier."

"I can answer that one," said Stephen. "At least I have a good idea. My brother worked as a postal worker for several years. I was once frustrated about a letter being 'lost' by the post office. So, I asked him what systems were in place to prevent letters being lost."

"He told me that as the letters get post marked, they are catalogued before they go through the sorting process. And the inventory is checked again after the letters are sorted to be sure nothing is missing. Phil must have smuggled the letters during the sorting process to make the copies."

"You're probably right," replied Jacob. "I guess he could have used a cell phone in the bathroom.

"So, Matt Baston's hatred of me reached a tipping point. He ordered Bubba, whom he had enticed with beer money to do his bidding in Columbia, to steal the letters as the post man was set to deliver them."

"But how did the letters end up in the old shack in the woods behind our house?" Tammy asked.

"I think I know that one," answered Peter. "As you know Bubba is soon to stand trial for Daniel's kidnapping. Alfred and I visited him several weeks ago. He's quite remorseful. In fact, I might even call him repentant. He can't believe how beer and sloth drove him to obey MB, as he calls him. Matt Baston convinced him that recapturing the letters was the thing to do for the greater good. Bubba didn't know what it was all about, but he knew that if he didn't steal the letters before they were delivered, MB would cut his beer money off.

"MB told him to destroy the letters, but in his curiosity, he slid them between the door planks in the old shack. He would often go to the shack to do what he wanted beyond his mother's nagging. So his intent was to read the letters later out of curiosity. But then he forgot about them. That is until he saw that the Eagan kids had found them."

"After Jacob and I broke up," Sarah continued. "I moved to Weed Drive, the street next to the Eagans. I wanted to be far removed from anyone who knew me. My mom came down to help me with Bryan's birth and stayed with me until the beginning of last year.

"I was not doing very well at all. My heart was aching. I couldn't get Jacob out of my mind. He'd called a couple of times, but left no message. I figured he'd moved on with his life. Baby Bryan constantly reminded me of Jacob and as hard as it is for me to admit, I needed a break from him."

"Mom agreed to keep Bryan in Greenville with her for a few months as long as I agreed to get some counseling. I said yes, but I never intended to get any counseling. How could a bunch of words heal a broken heart?"

"Matt must have had Bubba or somebody watch my house, because the day after mom moved out, he showed up.

"With all the charm he could muster, he convinced me that the girl I saw him with in Five Points was a passing fling and that he'd dreamed only of me. That he couldn't get me out of his mind since our days at the mental hospital.

"I believed him in my pain and agreed to move in with him. We stayed at one of his parents houses in the Shandon area on the other side of town.

"The first few months were really pretty good, but then I saw a shift in his whole demeanor. He stopped taking his medicine and began to talk about Jacob a lot. It was then that he told me about his friend at the Charleston Post

Office and about the Hope letter. Of course, he didn't mention Jacob's letter to me, but I could tell he was getting more and more anxious and fearful."

There was silence for a few moments as the last remaining dishes were cleared.

"Well to finish the story," Sarah continued. "Matt convinced me to come down here and live in this condo about a week before Daniel and Cassie found the letters. By then, I was ready to leave him, but his erratic behavior frightened me.

"I think Matt's plan was to move to Charleston so that he would be closer to Jacob and eventually kill him.

"I heard him threatening Bubba on the phone about the letters and from that moment on Matt was in full blown psychosis.

"And that is all I know," Sarah said, turning to her husband and smiling.

"Thank you Honey," Jacob stood up to address his guests. "I've learned a whole lot in this adventure. It's been extremely difficult at times, but now I couldn't be happier.

I may have wondered why my letters were stolen and why Daniel was kidnapped and why he and his family had to go through such frightening circumstances.

"However, I've had some long talks with my new dear friends Peter and Alfred. They helped me see, that even the difficulties we face are part of the tapestry of our lives. Threads are woven together to make us who we are, the good times and the bad.

"We don't always understand how our difficulties play a part in who we are, but I have a couple of conclusions about the grand adventure we've shared.

"Sarah recently told me that three years ago she was so angry at me she probably would have burned my letter unopened. However, because the letter was not delivered as I intended, she had three years to sort out how she really felt.

"In talking with Hank, I realized that Daniel's disappearance played a huge part in him coming to his sense and his family being reunited and healed.

"Hank, I understand you have your son back. Am I right?"

Hank's wiped his eyes and nodded.

"And all of us, in the adventure of a very strange weekend, are knitted together for life."

"There were many dark hours, but in the glimmer of the setting sun a lost letter was found, hearts were healed and families were reconciled."

"Let's all go forward from this place; encountering what awaits us with one resounding truth. No matter what happens; whether in this world or the next, hope remains."

Epilogue

Almost six months later at Peter's office at the University of South Carolina

"So you're sure you're through with it, Jimmy?" Peter joked, as Jimmy handed back his journal.

"Yea, I'm sure, Doc. I've learned all I can from our first adventure. I've kept it long enough. It's a good read. It really would make a great novel. I've started my own journal to document our adventure."

"Listen, Doc. Do you have a minute? I'd like to tell you what Stephen and I are thinking about next."

"Not really, Jimmy. I have to go. Alfred just called and he's asked me to come pick him up at his condo."

"But Doc! Did you know Stephen's found out in one of his grandfather's journals that he used to look at the sky a lot when he was in the Navy? And of course he knew Morse code. We know of a particular night before the Titanic …."

Peter kept walking toward the stair well as Jimmy's words faded.

About a half an hour later

"What this you said about leaving?" Peter said, as Alfred closed the passenger door.

"I'm considering it, Peter," Alfred admitted. "My lease is up next month and I'm thinking of moving back to Atlanta. A couple in the last church I was in could really use some help."

"But, you haven't made your final decision?" Peter asked.

"No, still praying."

"Well, to be honest. I'll be praying too. Praying that you'll stay," Peter said as he looked over at Alfred and smiled.

Peter shifted into drive and pulled out onto Laurel Street. "Where're we headed?"

"To the mental hospital."

"The mental hospital," Peter exclaimed. "Why are we going there?"

"I was hoping you would visit Matt Baston with me."

Made in the USA
Lexington, KY
01 April 2019